AS THE EARTH SPINS

EPISODE I:
THE DRAMA BEGINS

KARLTON CLAY

Edited by
Camille Allen

Expand Knowledge Publications
www.expandknowledge.net

As The Earth Spins

Episode 1:
The Drama Begins

By

Karlton Clay

ISBN 978-0-6151-7989-6

This book is in memory of:

My little sister Kristina Miracle Clay (WE LOVE YOU GIRL!)
My cousin & godfather Shedrick Moore
And My heart & grandmother Georgia Louise Bailey Morris

I would like to thank my Father in Heaven who is my Provider, Sustainer, Healer, Grace and Mercy-giver, and Forgiver; my Lord and Savior Jesus Christ for His selfless act of love for my sins on the cross; and the Holy Spirit that resides within me for comforting, inspiring, guiding, and correcting me.

And last but certainly not least, I would like to thank my family and friends for all of the love and support you give.

The winter of 2001

Tyreke and Eve Maxey walked around the empty house. This house had two stories and was quite huge. Tyreke and Eve were a young couple who just married a year ago. Eve was nine-months pregnant, and she could deliver her expectant son any day now.

"So, what do you think?" the young journalist asked his wife.

"I like it! I think this will be a perfect place for us to start our family."

"So, are we going to take it?" Tyreke asked Eve.

Before Eve could open her mouth to answer, the realtor strolled in with eagerness. "Well, what has our lovely couple decided to do?"

Tyreke glanced at Eve with a questionable expression, but Eve eased him with her smile. Tyreke looked at the realtor with a grin on his face and said, "We'll take it!"

The summer of 2006

Tyreke picked up his pen and signed on the dotted line. Tyreke's lawyer, Mr. Alan Barrette, picked up the papers and handed them to Judge Adam Taylor.

There was a dead silence in the courtroom as Tyreke, Mr. Barrette, and Eve, who set on the other end of the courtroom with her lawyer, waited on the judge's decision.

Judge Taylor banged his gavel on the stand. "Order! Order! I hereby declare this divorce approved and final! Case dismissed!"

Chapter 1

It was decided that TJ, Tyreke and Eve's five years-old son, would live with Tyreke on the weekdays and stay with Eve on the weekends. Tyreke also got the house. Eve did not mind because she did not want to be reminded of that failure called a marriage.

It was now August, and the night was cold and windy. Tyreke walked his date, Ida Freeman, to her front door. "I had a wonderful evening!" she said. Ida was very obsessed with Tyreke.

By the look on Tyreke's face, he was very uncomfortable about all of the attention she was giving him. "Look," Tyreke said while he was trying to stop Ida from rubbing his face, "I like you, but I think you are looking for a serious relationship. Am I right?"

"That's correct!" Ida said. "Tyreke, what are you trying to say?"

"I'm not ready for a serious relationship. I think it's better for me to let you know how I'm feeling now so you can look for someone else that feels about you the same way you feel about me."

"If that's what you want," Ida said trying to hold back her tears, "FINE! But you can't say I didn't try!" Ida opened the door and slammed the door in his face.

Eve was just wandering around the mall. She was thinking of everything going on right now in her life. Her life was in shackles. She did not know who or where to turn. So dazed by her confusion, Eve bumped into a young man. "Oh! Excuse me! I am so sorry!" Eve apologized. She was smiling to cover up her embarrassment.

"Wow!" the young man said in amazement.

"What?"

"Your smile. It's beautiful!"

"Thanks. That was the nicest compliment I've received in a long time!" Eve admitted. "Eve Maxey."

"I'm Sean Powers," he said as he took her hand and kissed it. "I'm sorry. I hope you don't think I was being forward."

"No, not at all."

"Well," Sean pulled out his card, "here's my card. Give me a call sometime."

"Okay, Sean." As Sean walked away, Eve glanced at the card. Maybe there was life after divorce.

Chapter 2

The phone rang the next day at Tyreke's house in the den. TJ was sitting on the couch, and he picked up the phone. "Hello?"

"Hey baby! How are you?"

"I'm doing fine, Mommy."

"Can I speak to your dad?"

"Sure," TJ said as he put the phone down. "Daddy! Telephone!"

Tyreke walked in from the kitchen. "Who is it?" he asked.

"Mama," TJ said as he hopped off the couch and walked into the kitchen.

Tyreke sighed and picked up the phone. "Hello?"

"Hey, Tyreke. Are you busy?" Eve asked seeming eager to talk to someone.

"No. What's up?"

"I just want to know if you think this divorce was the best thing to do. You know, I was thinking about TJ and the toll it'll have on him."

Tyreke knew it had to be more than that because this thought passed through his mind a lot as well. "I don't know."

"Oh." Eve seemed rather disappointed in the answer that he gave. "Well, I got to go. Bye."

"Bye."

Ding-dong! Tyreke got up and walked to the door to open it. He opened up the door, and a woman with a nine years-old girl was standing outside of the door. "Tonya?"

"Hey, Ty!" the young lady smiled.

"What are you doing here?" he asked.

Tonya Keller was an ex-girlfriend of Tyreke's in high school. "I have some news for you. This is Brianna...and she is your daughter."

Tyreke gasped.

Chapter 3

ve hung up the phone. She was not expecting the answer that she received from Tyreke. Eve noticed the card Sean had given her on the desk beside the phone. She picked it up and stared at it. Then, Eve did the only thing she could do; she picked up the phone and dialed the number.

The phone continued to ring. "Maybe he's not home," Eve said to herself.

Then the phone clicked, and a voice said, "Hello?"

"Hi. This is Eve," she answered. "May I speak to Sean?"

"This is he," Sean said happily on the other line. "Hey Eve! How are you doing?"

"I'm doing fine!" Eve smiled.

"Come on in," Tyreke said as Tonya and Brianna walked in the house. Tyreke closed the door. Brianna and Tonya sat down on the couch. "So, how did this happen?"

Brianna and Tonya looked at Tyreke. "Come on, Dad! I even know how it happened," Brianna remarked smartly.

"Dad," Tyreke said to himself. He said it as if he was mesmerized by the word.

TJ walked in from the kitchen smacking on a sour apple. "What's going on?" he asked.

"TJ, this is Brianna," Tyreke introduced, "your new sister."

"But Daddy, I thought for me to have a new baby sister," TJ innocently tried to explain, "she'd have to be a baby, and you'd have to be married to Mommy. Well, you're not married to Mommy anymore, and this girl is not a baby!"

"TJ, I'll explain it to you when you get a little bit older," Tyreke chuckled. Then, he turned to Brianna and Tonya and asked, "Would you two like to stay for dinner?"

Tonya stood up. "Well, I don't know. I have a lot of work to finish."

"Please?" TJ begged with innocence in his eyes.

"Can we, Mommy?" Brianna asked.

"Yeah," Tyreke begged imitating TJ and Brianna. "Mommy, can you stay?"

"Sure. Why not," Tonya finally answered. Tonya,

Brianna, TJ, and Tyreke walked in the kitchen with a gleam in their eyes and hunger in their stomachs.

Chapter 4

yreke attended The Pearly Gates Baptist Church. He was sitting on the steps of the church one windy afternoon with his two cousins, Tony Carter and Tyrone Carter, and his friend, Malik Anderson.

"So... now you are a father of two?" Malik asked.

"Yeah. She just came to my door two weeks ago and said this is your daughter Brianna."

"So, is Brianna going to stay with you?" Tyrone asked. He seemed concerned about the whole matter. He knew his cousin would need a little support.

"Yeah," Tyreke said, "she's going to stay with me for a little while so we can get to know each other."

Then, a loud, beeping noise sounded. Tony checked his beeper. "Oh, that was me."

"Who is it?" Tyrone asked his younger brother. Tyrone

was older than Tony by three years.

"It's Faith," Tony replied after checking his beeper. "She must be ready for our date tonight. Tyrone, we better get home." Faith Butler was Tony's long-committed girlfriend.

Tony and Tyrone began to walk to their apartment building, which was right around the corner from the church.

"Yeah," Malik said giving Tyreke dap. "I got to get to the house, too." Malik got in his car and drove off.

Tyreke began to walk to his car, but then a bluish-silver car drove up in front of the church. Then, a beautiful, young lady stepped out of her car. The young woman looked at Tyreke and asked, "Excuse me. Do you know if the pastor is here?"

Tyreke was amazed by her beauty. He could not speak. "Ah…ah…no, he's not here."

"Oh. Okay," the young lady said. "Thank you."

She began to get in her car, but Tyreke ran over to her. "Um… I didn't catch your name," he said.

"My name is Shawna Simmons," the young woman said. "And yours?"

"My name is Tyreke Maxey. Where do you live?"

"I live about an hour away from here," Shawna said.

"Maybe I could get your number, and we could get to know each other a little better," Tyreke suggested.

"I don't give my number to strangers," Shawna said. "How about we meet at a restaurant for dinner tomorrow night?"

"How about at *Ken's*?" Tyreke suggested. "My friend Malik owns the restaurant."

"Fine with me," Shawna said. "Is 7:30 okay with you?"

"See you then," Tyreke said.

Shawna got in her car and drove off. Tyreke smiled. *Man,*

I got some serious game!

There was a knock on the door of apartment 3B. Tonya opened the door, and a young man was standing at the door. "Taylor, what are you doing here?" Tonya asked.

"I am here for my daughter," Taylor Dunn answered in a demanding voice.

Chapter 5

"What are you talking about?" Tonya asked trying to pretend like she was confused.

"You know exactly what I'm talking about!" Taylor shouted. "I want to see my daughter!"

"If you're talking about Brianna, she's not here right now," Tonya said.

"Where is she?" Taylor asked in a calmer voice.

"She's over someone's house," Tonya answered.

"Whose house is she over?"

"A friend's," Tonya answered bluntly.

Taylor was getting restless. "Tonya, stop playing these games! Where is she?"

"She's over Tyreke's house!" Tonya finally gave in.

"Tyreke's house?" Taylor wondered. "How long has she been over there?"

"For about two weeks."

"And why is she over there for that long? Is something wrong with you? You sick?"

"No," Tonya replied. "It's just Tyreke and I agreed that Brianna should stay with him for a little while so that they can get to know each other better."

"And why would they want to get to know each other better…you know what! I'm sick of this! I want to know why my daughter is over Tyreke Maxey's house, and I want to know now!" Taylor demanded.

"Taylor," Tonya tried to explain, "right now, you are going through a tough time with your job and money, and she didn't know who her father was anyway even though you were paying child support. Brianna wanted to know who her father was, and I told her… that Tyreke was her father."

"So… you lied to Tyreke and OUR daughter!" Taylor exclaimed. "Why?"

"I don't know!" Tonya began to cry. She walked to her couch and sat down.

Taylor walked in, closed the door, and sat beside Tonya. "Look," Taylor calmly explained. "I love you, and I love our daughter. I want us to be together as a family. So… after you tell Brianna and Tyreke the truth, I want you and Brianna to move into my new house."

"Your new house?" Tonya questioned. Tonya's tears began to dry up. "What are you talking about?"

"I got a promotion at my job," Taylor answered.

"You did! Congratulations!" Tonya shouted.

Tonya gave Taylor a big hug and kiss. "But now YOU have something to take care of," Taylor told Tonya.

It had now been more than a month later since Tonya dropped the bomb on Tyreke that Brianna was his daughter. However, it seemed that Tyreke and TJ were now adjusting to having another person apart of their family. Tyreke and Malik were sitting on the couch watching the football game at Tyreke's house that Monday evening. Then, the doorbell rang. Brianna ran down from upstairs and opened the door. Eve was at the door.

"Excuse me," Brianna asked, "who are you?"

"I'm Eve," she replied, "may I ask who you are, little girl?"

"My name is Brianna," she answered. "I'm Tyreke's daughter."

"Daughter?" Eve exclaimed. "That's impossible!"

"Nothing's impossible," Brianna said as she walked back upstairs. Eve walked in and closed the door. She walked towards the couch.

"Tyreke, is that little girl really your daughter?" Eve asked.

"Is it any of your business?" Malik intervened.

"I don't think that I was talking to you," Eve snapped back. Malik and Eve always had confrontations with each other, but deep down inside, they cared about one another. "Anyway, like I was saying before I was so RUDELY interrupted, who is that little girl?"

"Brianna is really my daughter," Tyreke explained. "I found out about a month ago from her mother."

"And why wasn't I informed about this?" Eve asked feeling a little insulted.

"Again...because it is not any of your business," Malik interjected.

"Malik, please," Tyreke responded trying to keep the peace. "Eve, I honestly did not think to inform you because I did not think you would care."

"So, are you and Brianna's mother dating now?" Eve asked trying to be nosy.

"No," Tyreke answered. "I'm dating a young woman named Shawna. We've been going out and getting to know each other for about two weeks now."

Malik had to put his two cents in. "Yeah. She's as beautiful as an African princess."

"Oh," Eve replied. "How did you meet her, Tyreke?"

"She's a member of the church," Tyreke answered. "She lives an hour away."

"By the way," Malik asked Eve, "how are you and Sean doing?"

"Sean and I decided to see other people," Eve answered.

"Oh," Malik concluded, "he dumped you."

"Whatever!" Eve shouted.

"It's only been about a little more than a month. Why did you and Sean break up?" Tyreke asked Eve.

"It just wasn't working out," she answered. "We rushed into the relationship too soon. Maybe you should consider that with you and Shawna's relationship before---"

"Girl," Malik said, "you need to quit hatin' on Tyreke and Shawna's relationship. Everyone knows you want to get back with Tyreke, but it ain't happening!"

"Look, I'm just trying to help out a friend," Eve pitifully said as she stormed out the door.

Tyreke began to open his mouth to call out to her in order to make sure she was okay, but it was too late.

"Man, don't worry about her," Malik suggested.

Maybe there was some truth in what Eve was saying.

Chapter 6

en's was a jazzy restaurant that served a variety of foods. Malik owned *Ken's*, and he had a dream of one day having a chain of restaurants all over the United States.

The restaurant was packed just like it was every day. Ron Turtle was sitting at one of the tables. Ron also attended The Pearly Gates Baptist Church. He was eating a cheeseburger with fries smacking quite loudly clearly showing how well he was enjoying the food.

Ron just happened to take a break from eating and looked up. He saw Shawna walk in. "Hey, that's Shawna. That's Tyreke's girl," Ron said to himself.

Shawna sat with a guy who already had a table.

"Maybe that's her brother or cousin," Ron concluded to himself.

Then, Shawna and the guy began to kiss passionately on the lips.

"Maybe not," Ron said.

Tyreke was sitting on the couch watching TV. TJ and Brianna ran downstairs and over to the couch. "You two stop all that running!" Tyreke demanded.

TJ and Brianna stopped immediately. Then, there was a knock on the door. Brianna walked to the door and opened it. "Hey, Mommy!"

Tonya walked in the door. "Hey, baby," she greeted not as excited as Brianna.

"Hi, Ms. Tonya," TJ said.

"Hello," Tonya said to TJ.

"What's up, girl?" Tyreke said.

"Um… Tyreke, can I talk to you?" Tonya said. "Brianna, you need to stay, too."

"TJ, go upstairs to your room," Tyreke said.

"Awww.... man! I'm always left out of the important conversations!" TJ complained as he walked upstairs to his room.

Tonya made her way to a chair and sat down.

"Mom, what's going on?" Brianna asked as she sat down beside Tyreke on the couch.

Tonya began. "I don't know how to say this, but---"

"Mom," Brianna had cut Tonya off, "I think I know what

you're going to say. Tyreke, I know you are not my real father."

"What?" Tyreke asked in confusion.

"Baby, how did you find out?" Tonya asked Brianna.

"Well, one day when I was in your room, I knocked down some of your papers, and I saw my birth certificate. Under 'father' it had Taylor Dunn's name on the line," Brianna explained.

"Brianna, why didn't you tell me you knew all of this before me and you came over here a few weeks ago?" Tonya asked.

"I saw how happy you were when you thought I was going to meet Tyreke for the first time," Brianna answered.

"Well, your *real* father wants us to move in with him in his new house," Tonya said. "Is that okay with you?"

"Yeah," Brianna said, "but could I spend the night over here for one more night?"

"Is that okay with you, Tyreke?" Tonya asked.

"Sure," Tyreke said, but he was really speechless.

"Great! Thanks, Tyreke!" Brianna exclaimed as she ran upstairs.

"Tyreke, you've been awful quiet," Tonya observed. "Are you okay?"

"No, I'm not!" Tyreke shouted. "Tonya, you lied to me about something real serious. That ain't cool!"

"I know it wasn't," Tonya said. "And I'm real, real sorry."

"Tonya, I think you should leave," Tyreke suggested.

Tonya stood up and walked over to the door. She opened it and said, "I'll be back in the morning to get Brianna." Then, she walked out of the house closing the door behind her.

"This day could get no worse!" Tyreke said to himself.

Then, there was a knock on the door. Tyreke walked to the

door and opened it. "What's up, Ron?" he greeted.

Ron began to explain. "Tyreke, I was eating lunch at *Ken's*, and I saw Shawna kissing another guy. Look, I'm sorry. I just thought---"

"Thanks, Ron," Tyreke said pretending to be grateful, and he closed the door in Ron's face. Tyreke sat on the couch, picked up the phone, and dialed Shawna's number.

"Hello?" Shawna's voice answered on the other line.

Tyreke began to talk. "Hey Shawna. How are you? I think we need to talk."

Chapter 7

The next day, Tonya came by Tyreke's house and picked up Brianna. It had been two months since Tonya left with Brianna, and they moved in with Taylor. Tyreke also broke up with Shawna around the same time.

It was now the beginning of December. Tyreke was sitting in *Ken's* drinking hot chocolate with big, thick, fat marshmallows. Then, Gerald Clayton and Lindsay Carney walked in with a young boy. Gerald and Lindsay went to high school with Tyreke. Lindsay, Gerald, and the little boy sat at the table with Tyreke.

"Hey guys!" Tyreke greeted. "What's going on?"

"We found this little boy on the street," Lindsay answered.

"What's his name?" Tyreke asked.

"He won't tell us," Gerald replied.

Tyreke looked at the little boy. "Hi. My name is Tyreke. What's your name?"

The little boy continued to be silent. It was like someone sucked the life out of him. He sat there quietly observing his surroundings and observing these three people who were standing and sitting around him. *Where am I? Why am I with these strange people? I want my family.*

Tyreke pulled a marshmallow out of his hot chocolate with his spoon. "I'll give you this if you tell me your name."

The little boy took the marshmallow. He put the marshmallow in his mouth and chewed it up for a few seconds. After he swallowed it, he answered, "My name is John."

"How old are you?" Tyreke asked.

"I'm twelve."

"John, where are your parents?" Gerald asked.

"I don't know," John innocently answered.

"And do you live all by yourself on the streets?" Lindsay wondered.

"Yes."

"I can't believe they left this innocent little kid on the streets all alone," Tyreke commented.

"Guys, we have to do something," Lindsay said.

"We need to call child services," Tyreke advised.

"I'll take care of it," Gerald said as he pulled out his cell phone and walked over to the counter.

While Gerald was asking the bartender for a telephone book, Lindsay said to Tyreke, "Well, he needs to stay somewhere until child services takes care of the situation."

"What are you suggesting?" Tyreke wondered.

Lindsay turned to John and looked him in the eyes lovingly as if with motherly compassion. "John, how would you like to stay with me for a little while?" she asked him.

John sat there for a minute and contemplated what she asked him. He did not really know this woman, but a place to stay is better than sleeping on the cold streets. "I'd like that," John replied.

"C'mon," Lindsay said, "let's go home!"

As she was walking out, Lindsay signaled over to Gerald that she was taking John to her apartment, and Lindsay and John walked out of *Ken's* happily. Lindsay had a warm feeling in her heart because she took the time to help someone, and John was grateful that he had somewhere to rest his head for the night.

Tyreke and TJ walked in Tyreke's house. "Did you enjoy yourself at Mom and Dad's?" Tyreke asked TJ.

"Yeah," TJ said. "I especially had fun watching Grandpa snore."

There was a knock on the door. Tyreke and TJ were all ready standing at the door so Tyreke opened it.

"Brianna," Tyreke said sounding surprised. "Tonya, what are you doing here?"

"Tyreke, can we talk?" Tonya asked.

Tyreke honestly did not know what to make of what she just said. After the last time she "needed to talk," he found out that Brianna was not really his child. His flesh wanted to slam the door in her face, but his conscience got the best of him allowing him to invite them in.

A few minutes later, Tonya and Tyreke were sitting at the table in the kitchen drinking coffee. "So," Tyreke asked, "how are you doing?"

"Well, as soon as Brianna and I moved in with Taylor, he began to change. He would always come home late and drunk. I would've moved out sooner, but I had to consider Brianna's feelings. She seemed so happy to have FINALLY met and be with her natural father, but I was seeing a side of him that Brianna didn't see. So, I finally decided to talk to him about it. We got in a big argument, and I broke up with him."

"Good for you," Tyreke complimented trying to be supportive.

"But in result of dumping him, he kicked me out of his house," Tonya added.

"Did he kick Brianna out, too?" Tyreke asked.

"No," Tonya said. "He said that she could stay with him, but I didn't want Brianna to be around Taylor when he's in his drunken state."

"So… now you're homeless?" Tyreke asked.

"Yeah. I guess you could say that."

"I know that two months ago when you told me that Brianna wasn't my daughter, I lost all responsibilities as a father to her, but for the moment that she's lived with me and TJ, I really got to know her as my daughter. While Brianna was gone for these past two months, even though she isn't, I still considered her as my daughter. I haven't, won't, and never will turn my back on TJ… and I won't do it to Brianna or her mother either."

"Tyreke, what are you saying?" Tonya asked.

"You and Brianna can move in with us," Tyreke said.

"Thank you, Tyreke!" Tonya gratefully said. "Thank you

so much!"

"Do you have any bags?" Tyreke asked.

"They're in the car," Tonya answered.

"I'll get those out later," Tyreke responded, "after I take you, Brianna, and TJ out to dinner."

Tyreke and Tonya began to smile. Tyreke was grateful that he had his "daughter" back.

Chapter 8

ve was an assistant fashion designer at *Chico's*, which was owned by the outlandish, Spanish designer Alvin J. Chico. She was an excellent designer and designed at least fifty of the outfits for *Chico's*.

It was around Christmas time, and Eve was sitting at her desk drawing a new outfit to show Mr. Chico. Then, a door slammed. Eve knew it was from Mr. Chico's office because his office was north of her desk. Eve turned around, and she saw a man with a bandana on his head walking out of Mr. Chico's office. He was very dark-skinned, and he looked as if he was upset with Mr. Chico.

The young man walked to Eve's desk. "Can you believe that fool?" he asked. "He didn't give me a job."

"Did he tell you why he didn't?" Eve asked trying to be courteous to this stranger.

"It was for something stupid," he said.

"Well, what was the reason?"

He answered hesitantly, "Because I didn't finish school."

"Do you mean college?"

"No," the young man answered. "I mean high school."

"Oh," Eve said dumbfounded.

"So," the young man began to recognize Eve's beauty, "what do you like in a man?"

"I'd have to know his name," Eve smiled.

"My name is Artie Bush," he said. "And yours?"

"Eve," she smiled again.

"Well, we could be like Adam and Eve," Artie joked.

Eve replied, "I don't think so."

"Can we go out one night?" Artie anxiously asked.

"Artie," Eve had to put him down gently, "I'm sorry, but I don't date people I don't know."

"Oh." Artie softly said as he began to walk away.

"Wait!" Eve shouted. Artie turned around and ran back to Eve's desk. "What are you doing on New Year's Eve?" she asked.

"Nothing," Artie responded. "Why?"

"Well, my church holds a *Watchnight* service; we have a church service on New Year's Eve at church at 10:30 PM until 12:01 of the new year," Eve explained. "Would you like to come with me?"

"Sure," Artie said. "It's not a date, but at least I'll be with you."

"Here is the address to my church," Eve said writing down the address to Pearly Gates Baptist Church and handing it to Artie. "I'll see you at 10:00 PM on New Year's Eve."

"I'll see you there," he said as he grabbed the sheet of paper and suavely walked out the door.

It seemed as if it was just a few seconds before New Year's Eve came, and just as Eve said, The Pearly Gates Baptist Church held their annual *Watchnight*.

It was 10:30 on the dot that night. The pews were so crowded that they had to put chairs in the aisles. Tyreke, Tyrone, Tony, and three lovely young ladies – Denise West, Kellie Rush, and Cherie Rush – were sitting on the last pew on the right side of the church. "Where's Faith?" Tyreke leaned over and asked Tony.

"She had to work," Tony replied.

Denise dipped into the conversation between them. "She had to work on New Year's Eve?"

"Yeah," Tony said. "My baby is a business woman."

"So… basically, she makes more money than you," Tyrone jived.

"Don't hate because you ain't got no woman," Tony responded.

"I won't have to worry about that soon," Tyrone said looking over and smiling at Denise. "Right, Denise?"

"Boy, you need to stop!" Denise laughed.

Tyreke looked at his watch. "I wonder where my parents and my siblings are," Tyreke said to himself. Tyreke searched and searched until he finally spotted them. Tyreke's dad, Rev. Avery

Maxey, was sitting on the pulpit with the other associate minister and the pastor. Tyreke's mom, Mrs. Maxine Maxey, was sitting with her sister, Ms. Allison Johnson. Tyreke's two youngest siblings, Skeeter Maxey and Grace Maxey, were sitting with Mrs. Maxey as well. Tyreke's two sisters, Mary Maxey and Kayla Maxey, were sitting in the choir stand with the other choir members.

Then, Malik walked in and sat beside Tyreke. "What's up, man?" Malik greeted.

"Why you so late?" Tyreke asked.

"I had to close out the restaurant for the holidays," Malik said. "Where's TJ?"

"My Aunt Cecelia is babysitting him," Tyreke said. Cecelia Nixon was Mrs. Maxey's other sister.

Then, Eve and Artie walked in. Tyreke, Malik, Tony, Tyrone, Denise, Cherie, and Kellie looked at them with shock and curiosity. "Why are they staring at me?" Artie asked.

"Don't worry about it," Eve said. "Let's just sit down." They sat directly in front of where Tyreke, Malik, Tony, Tyrone, Denise, Cherie, and Kellie were sitting.

Cherie leaned to the front and whispered to Eve, "Who is that man with you?"

"His name is Artie," Eve whispered back.

"Where did you meet him?" Cherie asked.

The service began to start. "I'll talk to you later," Eve responded.

As the choir began to sing, the Spirit of God filled the sanctuary. Everyone was having such a good time in the Lord that no one was aware that an hour and a half had passed. "All right everyone!" Pastor Bruce announced. "It is 12:01! Happy New

Year!"

The church shouted and cheered with praise. Pastor Bruce began again, "Now if you want to start the New Year off right with our Lord and Savior, Jesus Christ, you can join me in front of this altar right now."

The choir began to hum "Come to Jesus." Artie leaned over to Eve. "So, do you like a Christian man?" he asked.

"Yeah," Eve said. "I would like to have one."

Artie stood up. "This is for you, babe." He walked down the aisle and to the altar. As the church applauded in support, a deacon stood behind him in support of him.

"Or you can rededicate your life to Him," Pastor Bruce said. "You can start over with Him and recommit your life to Him."

Denise turned to Tyrone. "Will you go up there with me?" she asked.

"I'll do anything for you," Tyrone said as he and Denise stood up and walked to the altar as the church praised God for two more people rededicating their lives to Christ.

Tyreke was thinking. He needed to reconnect with Christ. Maybe he could go through the things in his life that caused him strife and confusion with peace knowing that God was by his side. So, Tyreke boldly stood up and walked to the altar. As the church clapped and continued to praise God, in support, Tony and Malik stood up, walked to the altar, and stood behind Tyreke.

"Heaven is rejoicing now!" Pastor Bruce said as more and more people came to the altar.

The new year would be started off right.

Chapter 9

yreke worked at *The Boss Chronicle* as one of the head journalists. After *Watchnight*, these days Tyreke went to work and approached his fellow employees with a new attitude. Tyreke had just returned to work after a two-week vacation. He was sitting at his desk writing an article for the paper. Mr. Boss, the editor and the owner of *The Boss Chronicle*, had an office next to Tyreke's desk.

Mr. Boss stepped out of his office and towards Tyreke's desk. "Ty, could I see you in my office?"

Tyreke sat in the wooden chair in front of Mr. Boss' desk. Mr. Boss sat at his desk in his soft, leather reclining chair. "What did you want to talk about?"

"Well, me and the missus have decided to take a long missionary trip around South Africa," Mr. Boss said.

"That's great, sir," Tyreke said. Then, he asked, "What's

that got to do with me?"

"As I said, we might be gone for a long time, and I will not be able to fulfill my duties as editor while I'm away," Mr. Boss said. "So… I'm asking if you would like to fulfill the role as editor?"

"Yes, sir! I'd love to!" Tyreke excitedly accepted shaking Mr. Boss' hand.

"My son, Aaron, will be coming by a few days a week to check on the place to make sure everything is in order," Mr. Boss informed Tyreke.

"Okay," Tyreke said. "I won't let you down."

"I know you won't," Mr. Boss smiled as Tyreke joyfully walked out of his office.

Eve walked into her apartment tired from work. She sold at least six of her designs to Mr. Chico today. Eve threw her purse, brief-case, and coat on the floor and plopped down on the couch sitting next to the telephone. She reached over to the answer machine and pushed *play* on the machine.

Beep! "Hey girl! It's me! I was just checking to see if you got home yet. Give me a call when you get in." *Beep!*

Oh no! Eve thought. Eve rolled her eyes and blew her breath. *Artie has been calling my house for the past week non-stop. I have to get rid of him somehow*, Eve thought trying to think of a polite way to do it.

As she was thinking, the phone rang. Eve looked over the arm of the couch and at the Caller I.D. *BUSH, ARTIE* was across the I.D. screen.

"I think I'm going to go wash my hair," Eve said, and as she got up and walked to her room, the telephone continued to ring.

Chapter 10

ver since Gerald and Lindsay found young John on the streets, he had been staying with Lindsay. After child services came and took the case, they made an arrangement for Lindsay to be John's foster mother. It was now February, and John had been living with Lindsay for three months now. Lindsay was a medical student at Clayton University. She worked at the Clayton University Student Union as an assistant manager. Her goal was to become a pediatric nurse, but she had dreams and aspirations of becoming a model. Lindsay was a tall, beautiful woman who had done a couple of modeling jobs in her hometown.

Lindsay was sitting on the couch reading a *Beautiful* magazine. John had walked in the apartment with his book bag on his back. "What's up, Lindsay?" he greeted closing the door.

"Hey, John!" Lindsay said. "How was school today?"

"It was fine. In science class, we started our science fair projects."

"Do you have a partner?"

"Yeah," John replied. "His name is Terry. Is it okay if I go over his house this weekend to work on this project?"

"Yeah. That's fine," Lindsay said as John walked in the backroom. As Lindsay picked up her magazine, the telephone rang.

She picked it up. "Hello?" she answered.

"Hi. Is this Lindsay Carney?" the voice asked. It sounded like a middle-aged man.

"Yes," she replied. "This is her."

"My name is Amos Wilson. I am the dean of external affairs at Clayton University," he said. "I am aware that you are the assistant manager of the Student Union on campus. Is that correct?"

"Yes, sir, that is right," Lindsay said as she changed her position on the couch.

"Well, the manager of the Student Union, just came in my office and quit," Dean Wilson said. "I was just calling to see if you would be interested in being promoted to the position of manager of the Student Union. Do you accept the position?"

"I do!" Lindsay said as if she was getting ready to kiss her groom.

"Excellent!" Dean Wilson said. "I'll see you in the morning."

Then, Lindsay heard a click on the other line, and she hung up the phone. *I can't believe I'm the new manager of the Student Union*, she thought.

Just as she was thinking, a knock on her door interrupted

her thoughts. Lindsay got up and opened the door.

A tall, dark, middle-aged woman was standing at the door "May I help you?" Lindsay asked.

"I believe you can," she said. "My name is Delores Banks. I am looking for John Banks. He's my son."

Tyreke was sitting alone at a table in *Ken's* drinking an orange soda. While he was drinking, for some odd reason, he began to think about Ida. The last time he saw her was on their last date. *I wonder how she's doing*, Tyreke thought to himself.

Then, Tyreke heard laughing and giggling as if two people were on a date. As Tyreke turned around, he saw something totally shocking. Gerald and Ida were the couple laughing and giggling. They were laughing as if they were having a good time. *My friend is out with someone I used to date*, he thought. *Maybe I should say hello.*

Tyreke stood up and walked over to their table. "Hi," he said.

Ida looked up with a shocked expression on her face.

Gerald began to smile, and he greeted, "What's up man! Ida, this is my good friend, Tyreke. Tyreke, this is my new girlfriend, Ida."

Ida confessed, "I already know Tyreke."

"You do?" Gerald innocently asked. "How?"

"We used to date," Tyreke replied.

"Oh," Gerald responded. "Well, maybe we should get going."

"Okay," Ida agreed.

"It was nice to see you again, Ida," Tyreke smiled.

"Yeah," Ida said, "whatever."

"See you later," Gerald said to Tyreke as he and Ida walked out of the restaurant.

Tyreke pulled out his cell phone out of his breast pocket and dialed a phone number.

"Hello?" the female voice answered.

"Hey," Tyreke said. "My parents are going to watch TJ tonight. How would you like to go out to dinner?"

"I'd love to," the female voice said.

"Meet me at the French restaurant on 5th and Asian," Tyreke said.

"Okay," she said. "See you tonight."

Tyreke and the mysterious female hung up the phone at the same time.

Chapter 11

The next morning, Lindsay was sitting at the table in her mother's house in the kitchen sipping a cup of hot coffee. As she was drinking the coffee, she began to think. Then, the tears began to flow from her eyes.

"LINDSAY!" Mrs. Carney, Lindsay's mother, called from the living room. "You have a visitor here to see you!"

"I'm in the kitchen!" Lindsay shouted as she wiped her eyes.

She continued to sip her coffee as Gerald walked in as if he lost his best friend. "Hi," he said sadly as he sat at the table with her.

"Why do you look so sad?" Lindsay asked.

"Well, I was on a date with Ida last night," Gerald explained, "and we went to *Ken's*. Well, we bumped into Tyreke, and as I was introducing Ida to him, I found out that they use to date. Well, I thought it would be best if I would go ahead and take her home. When we arrived in front of her front door, out of the blue, she broke up with me. She said when she saw Tyreke again, old feelings began to surface, and she thought it would be wrong to lead me on. And then she said something that a man never wants to hear. *We can still be friends!*"

"I'm so sorry," Lindsay said trying to hold back her tears. She had problems of her own.

"Hey," Gerald observed, "have you been crying?"

"How could you tell?" Lindsay asked.

"Your eyes are a little puffy," Gerald replied. "What happened?"

"Well, last night the dean of external affairs of Clayton University called and gave me the job as manager of the Student Union."

"That's great!" Gerald exclaimed.

"That's where I'm supposed to be in a few minutes," Lindsay said. "But that's not why I was crying. Well, after the call, there was a knock on the door. I opened it, and a Ms. Delores Banks was at the door. She claimed to be John's mother. So, I checked it out with child services, and it was true.

"So, why did she abandon him?" Gerald wondered.

"Well, she explained that she and John were separated after her husband was killed. John's father was involved with drugs and was a drug dealer. After a bad drug bust, John's father was deeply in debt to the drug lord. One night, the drug lord demanded his money and threatened that if he did not have it that he would kill him, John's mother, and John. Well, John's father did not have the money, and the drug lord killed him. John's mother and John tried to escape, and I guess by the way she tells it, they were somehow separated. She claims that she's been searching for him ever since then. So, naturally, child services believed her story and agreed with her situation, and John went home with his real mother this morning."

Lindsay began to cry harder than she had ever cried before. Gerald tried to comfort her by putting his arms around her, but Lindsay broke free. "I have to go," she said as she popped out her seat, grabbed her purse, and walked out the back door.

Tyreke and Eve were sitting at the table in the kitchen in Tyreke's house. They were drinking water and laughing. "Thank you for having dinner with me last night," Tyreke said.

"You're welcome," Eve said. "That's what friends are for."

"We should go out as friends more often," Tyreke suggested.

"You know," Eve replied, "we have more fun now than we did when we were married."

"Here's a suggestion," Tyreke said. "How about we go out for dinner on Valentine's Day?"

"I'd love to," Eve said as she stood up. "Well, I have to get to work."

Eve put her jacket on, and she walked out the back door.

Tyreke stood up from the table and walked into the living

room. To his surprise, he saw Tonya kissing a guy on the couch. She seemed to not have noticed that Tyreke was standing at the door.

The guy just happened to look up, and immediately, he and Tonya stopped kissing. "Uh… baby, look behind you," he whispered.

Tonya turned around a saw Tyreke standing at the door as if he was waiting for an explanation. "Oh," Tonya embarrassingly replied. "Hi, Tyreke."

"Hey, Tonya," Tyreke smiled. "What's up, Ray! I'm sorry. I didn't know I would be interrupting something serious in my own house. I'll leave you guys alone."

He walked upstairs. Tonya had been dating Ray Bailey ever since she and Brianna moved back in with Tyreke and TJ.

"You know," Ray concluded, "Tyreke has a point."

"What do you mean?" Tonya asked.

"He said he'd never thought he would be interrupting something in his own house. He's right! He shouldn't have to worry about giving someone privacy in his own home."

"Ray," Tonya confusedly asked, "what are you saying?"

"I know it's only been a short time, but you know I love you," Ray replied. "And you know I'm crazy about Brianna. I want you two to move in with me."

Tonya sat on the couch stunned. She was thinking about why she and Brianna were living with Tyreke in the first place. Then, it hit her. The reason why they were living there was because she moved in with Taylor, Brianna's natural father, and they moved out because of his drinking habits. "I don't know," she finally replied.

"What's the problem?" Ray eagerly asked.

"I don't want to rush into anything," Tonya replied.

"Well, I don't want to put any pressure on you," Ray said as he stood up. "Just call me when you decide."

Ray put on his coat and kissed her on her lips. He walked towards the door, opened it, and walked out. Tonya sat on the couch thinking. *Do I want to make the same mistake again?*

Chapter 12

That night, Brianna was sitting in her room half-sleep with her neon green night-light. Tonya cracked the door open to see if her daughter was asleep.

The bright light from the hallway shined on Brianna's round face. She sat up and asked, "Is that you, mommy?"

Tonya walked in and sat on Brianna's bed. "Yeah. It's me!"

"What's wrong?" Brianna innocently asked.

"Do you like Ray?" Tonya asked Brianna.

"Yeah," she replied. "He's pretty cool. Do you like him?"

"I like him a whole lot," Tonya responded. Then she asked, "How would you feel if we – as in me and you – were to move in with him?"

"That's fine. But..."

"But what?" Tonya insistently asked. "Go ahead, baby.

Express how you feel."

"We're just moving so much," Brianna said. "First, I stayed with Tyreke. Then, we moved in with Daddy, and now we're back here living with Tyreke and TJ."

"So, I guess you don't want to move," Tonya said.

"No," Brianna said, "I don't mind moving. I just don't want to lose the relationship I have with Tyreke."

"You won't lose your relationship with him," Tonya said. "We can always come to visit."

"I would feel better if I could talk to Tyreke about this, too," Brianna replied.

"Maybe, I'll call a house meeting tomorrow night," Tonya responded. This was a big issue that affected everyone in the house.

Tyreke walked in *The Boss Chronicle* office the next morning with his head held high. It had been a month since Mr. Boss left for South Africa and Tyreke became the editor. The office ran smoothly, and everyone had a smile on their face.

Tyreke placed his suitcase on his desk. Francis McMillan, Tyreke's old high school classmate and his assistant editor, walked up to him. "Good morning, sir," she greeted.

"Hey, girl!" Tyreke replied. "What's up?"

"Nothing really," Francis said. She picked up this morning's newspaper off of Tyreke's desk. "This paper is excellent! You did a great job!"

"No," Tyreke humbly responded, "*we* did a great job."

The elevator bell rang, and the doors opened. Aaron Boss and his sister, Amy Boss, walked out of the elevator and stormed towards Tyreke and Francis.

Aaron snatched the newspaper out of Francis' hand. "What in the world is this?" Aaron shouted.

"I think it's a newspaper," Amy sarcastically said, "but I could be wrong."

"No, it's not!" Aaron replied. "It's a piece of trash!"

"Well, no one else is complaining," Francis responded to Aaron's ignorance.

"What's the matter with it?" Tyreke calmly asked trying not to get upset.

"Why are there word finds, crosswords, cartoons, and comic strips in this paper?" Aaron asked.

"I put it in the paper for the kids," Tyreke replied. "The newspaper will *finally* attract a younger audience.

"A newspaper is for news; not junk," Aaron responded. "And that is exactly what this is: JUNK!" He slammed the newspaper on the floor.

"Well, we've been doing this ever since Mr. Boss left for South Africa," Francis said. "It's been a month. Why haven't you come up here before?"

"He's been in therapy," Amy snickered.

"My personal and private business is not the issue here," Aaron responded trying to change the subject back to the newspaper. "The issue is that I demand you to stop with the excess and stick with the news."

"Well, I do believe that your father put me in charge," Tyreke said, "and I make the decisions around here. The *excess* stays."

"I guess he told you!" Amy laughed.

"Okay," Aaron warned, "you may have got me this time, but I can promise you that we will meet again."

"Looking forward to it," Francis sarcastically said.

Aaron walked to the elevator and pressed the down-arrow button.

"Keep up the good work," Amy said as she ran to the elevator before the doors closed.

"Well," Tyreke said, "back to work!"

Chapter 13

Brianna, TJ, and Ray were sitting on the couch watching cartoons that afternoon. Suddenly, the door opened, and Tyreke walked in. "Hey guys," he greeted as he closed the door.

"Hi," TJ and Brianna responded as they continued to have their eyes glued to the television.

"Do you know what's going on?" Ray asked Tyreke.

Tyreke walked over to a chair and sat down. "What are you talking about?"

"Well, Tonya called me at work and told me as soon as I get off to come over here."

Tonya walked out of the kitchen. She observed that everyone was in the room. Smiling, she said, "Good. Now everyone is here!"

"What's this about?" Tyreke asked with a puzzled look on

his face.

"Okay," Tonya began to explain. She was so excited that she could not just sit down. "As you all know, I have been dating Ray for quite a while now, and I am very much in love with him. He's very good with Brianna, and he takes very good care of us."

Ray cracked a big smile.

"But what does this have to do with me and TJ?" Tyreke asked.

"Well, you have been so gracious by opening your home up to me and my daughter. But I think it is time for me to leave now. You need your privacy, and so do I."

"Where are you going to stay?" TJ asked. He was very concerned of the well-being of Tonya and especially Brianna since she was like a sister to him.

"Well," Tonya began again, "Ray has invited me and Brianna to live with him."

TJ turned to Brianna with innocence in his eyes. "But you're my friend. I don't want to lose you."

"You won't lose me," Brianna said. "We'll always be friends." Brianna and TJ gave each other a big hug.

"So, what are you going to do?" Tyreke asked.

"I have decided to move in with Ray," Tonya replied.

"Yes!" Ray shouted as Tonya ran to him, and they shared a passionate kiss.

Eve looked around in her apartment. It was quiet as a deserted ghost town. She needed some joy and fulfillment in her life. Then, she thought of a solution. Eve jumped to the couch and dialed Tyreke's phone number on the phone.

"Hello?"

"Hi, Tyreke! Look, I was just wondering if TJ could come live with me for a while."

Chapter 14

During the next two days, Brianna and Tonya made their transition from Tyreke's house to Ray's condominium. The next day, Eve came and picked up TJ. Now, the loneliness in her life was sort-of filled.

That morning, Tyreke walked into his parents' house as if he still lived there. "Don't you ever knock?" his sister Kayla asked. That was her way of saying hello.

"Hello to you, too," Tyreke said as he hugged his outspoken sister.

Tyreke's brother, Skeeter, was sitting on the couch watching the game on TV. He did not even notice that Tyreke walked into the room. "Hello, Skeeter," Tyreke greeted.

Silence. "I said hello!" Tyreke repeated. Still silence. Tyreke had a plan to get Skeeter to speak to him. "Kayla," he began, "you'll never believe that fine honey I saw on the street before I came here."

Skeeter jumped up and shouted, "Where?"

"Good job! You got his attention," Kayla said.

"Y'all tricked me!" Skeeter said.

"Yep," Tyreke and Kayla said in unison.

"Don't talk to me!" Skeeter pouted as he sat back down on the couch.

Just then, Mrs. Maxine Maxey and Tyreke's youngest sister, Grace, walked in from the kitchen. "Tyreke!" Mrs. Maxey shouted.

"Mom!" Tyreke greeted back as he hugged his loving mother.

"What do you want?" Grace asked.

"Can't I come visit my family without wanting anything?" Tyreke asked.

Everyone, except Mrs. Maxey, replied, "No!"

"What's up?" Mrs. Maxey asked.

"I was just so lonely in that big house now that TJ is staying with Eve and that Tonya and Brianna has moved in with Ray," Tyreke confessed. "Where's Dad?"

"Avery is at the church because Pastor Bruce called an auxiliary leaders meeting," Mrs. Maxey said.

Then, the front door opened, and Mary Maxey rushed into the living room from outside like a speeding bullet. "This is awful!" she exclaimed.

"Well, hello to you, too," Tyreke smiled.

"What's wrong, sweetie?" Mrs. Maxey asked with concern.

"Well, you know our sorority shares our house with our sisters at Clayton University, which is built right by their campus," Mary explained. She attended Universal Medical College. "Well, this semester, the campus population has at least tripled. And they claim to need more parking spaces. Since the university owns the sorority house, the executives of the university can do whatever they want with it. So, they've decided to tear it down to make more parking spaces."

"That's terrible!" Mrs. Maxey exclaimed.

"Do you have anywhere to stay?" Grace asked.

"No," Mary replied.

"So, most likely you'll be moving back home," Skeeter concluded. He just happened to stop focusing his attention on the game to come in on the tail end of Mary's explanation.

Then, a light bulb clicked on in Tyreke's head. "Hey," he said, "maybe I can donate my house and you could move in."

"What?" Mary asked in confusion.

"Well, it doesn't make any sense for me to have a big house anymore since TJ, Brianna, and Tonya don't stay with me now."

"But where are you going to stay?" Mrs. Maxey asked.

"I'll find me an apartment," he responded.

"Thanks, big bro!" Mary exclaimed. "I can't wait to tell the other girls! How can we ever repay you?"

"By having my rent at the end of each month!" Tyreke replied.

Lindsay was sitting on the couch watching television. Then, she glanced at the table across the room. There was a picture of her and her boyfriend, William Banks. She met William at the club the day she told Gerald about John's mother coming to get her son; they began to go out in order to get to know each other the next day. Since then, they have been dating and enjoying each other's company. It seemed that the hole in Lindsay's heart from losing John was not as deep as it was before she started dating William.

As she was reminiscing, there was a knock on the door. Lindsay stood up and opened the door. "William!" she greeted as he walked in.

"Um… I have to ask you something," William replied.

"What is it?"

"I know that we have not been seeing each other for that long, but I've never felt this way about any other woman I've been with. I knew it was love at first sight when I first saw your beautiful face more than a month ago. I know that it's only been a month and some change, but I believe that when it's right, it's right." William pulled out a box and opened it to reveal a sparkling, diamond ring. He got on one knee and asked, "Will you marry me?"

Chapter 15

"So?"

"Yes, I'll marry you!" Lindsay shouted as William put the ring on her finger, and they shared a passionate kiss.

Eve walked to her desk with a smile on her face. The receptionist walked over to her and responded, "You have a visitor."

She walked away as Artie walked to her desk. "Hello, Artie," Eve smiled.

"Well, you are the cheerful one," Artie said. "What crawled up your panties this morning?"

"The happy bug, I guess."

"Well, I want you to meet a good friend of mine." Then, he called, "George! Get over here!"

If George is anything like Artie, then I don't want to meet him, she thought trying to maintain a smile on her face.

As George walked over, he seemed to be the exact opposite of Artie. He was quiet, neat, and poised. He had a wonderful smile. Then, after Eve was checking George out, their eyes made contact.

Unaware of what was going on, Artie began the introductions. "George, this is my close and personal friend, Miss Eve Maxey. Eve, this is George Fryer, Jr. He's a computer research engineer. And of course, y'all know me." He laughed at his own joke.

Eve and George lightly chuckled, but not at Artie's joke.

Artie looked at his watch. "Oh no! I have to be getting to work. C'mon, George! We have to go!"

"It was nice meeting you," George said still smiling.

"Same here," Eve replied.

George and Artie walked out of the building, but every opportunity he got, George kept looking back at Eve. As he continued to sneak a peak at her, Eve continued to flash the perfect smile.

Lindsay, her mother, Mrs. Ruth Carney, and her brother, Josh Carney, were sitting on the couch. "Congratulations on your engagement to William!" Mrs. Carney said. "That ring is beautiful!"

"I know," Lindsay bragged. "William and I decided not to have a long engagement, and we decided to speed up the moving process so I'm going to go ahead and move some of my things into William's apartment."

"Do you need any help?" Josh asked.

"We might," Lindsay answered.

"Well, don't call me!" Josh replied and began to laugh, but no one else did. Then, he got up and began walking towards the kitchen. "I think I'm going to give Will a call."

"Why?" Lindsay asked.

"To give him my sympathy!" Josh guffawed all the way into the kitchen.

"So, have you told Gerald about this engagement?" Mrs. Carney asked.

"No," Lindsay answered. "Why are you bringing him up?" Even though, she knew what her mother was driving at.

"You know that Gerald has these *feelings* for you. He has for a very long time."

"And he knows that I'm dating William and he knows how serious we are."

"But still---"

"I know, Ma."

"So, how are you going to go about telling Gerald the news?"

"I don't know," Lindsay replied.

Chapter 16

Eve and TJ walked into the apartment that afternoon. "So, how was school today?" she asked her son.

"It was good," TJ said. Then, he remembered, "My teacher said don't forget to bring a class set of Valentine's Day cards tomorrow."

"Will do," Eve laughed. Then, the telephone rang. She picked it up and answered, "Hello?"

"Is this Eve?" the voice on the other line asked.

"Yes, this is she. May I ask whose calling?"

"This is George. Remember from the other day?

"George! Hi! Not to be rude, but how did you get my phone number?"

"I looked it up in the phone book. I hope you don't mind."

"No, as a matter of fact, I don't," Eve replied in embarrassment. "So, what do I owe the pleasure of your call?"

"What are you doing for Valentine's Day?" he asked.

"Nothing. Why?"

"How would you like to go out with me tomorrow night?"

"I'd love to," Eve quickly answered. "Let me find a sitter for my son, and I'll call you back."

"How are you going to call me back when you don't even have my number?" George responded.

"I have Caller I.D.," she replied.

"Oh." Now, he was the one feeling a little embarrassed. "I'll stay right here by the phone waiting for your call."

"Okay. Bye." She hung up the phone smiling and laughing. Suddenly, the laughter stopped. She forgot about one thing – the "date" she all ready made with her ex-husband.

Gerald was sitting at a table in *Ken's* eating his ham sandwich. As he was eating, Lindsay began to pop in his mind. Gerald was so drawn by her enchanting beauty, sparkling personality, quick wit, and sharp intelligence. Lindsay was the girl of his dreams.

Anthony walked out of the men's restroom and sat down at the table with Gerald. "I feel ten pounds lighter!" he said sighing.

Gerald pushed his plate aside. "Thank you for ruining my appetite," he moaned.

Lindsay walked in, and she noticed Gerald and Anthony sitting at a table. She had to tell him. She had to tell Gerald about her and William's engagement. Lindsay walked over to the table and greeted, "Hi, guys."

"Lindsay," Gerald joyfully greeted, "Hi. I'm glad you're here. Do you have any plans for tomorrow?"

"Well, see…"

He cut her off. "I was thinking that maybe me and you could have a Valentine's Day dinner."

"Gerald, I have something to tell you," she replied.

"What?" he asked.

"Well… um… I'm sorta… kinda… actually I am engaged to William."

Gerald paused for a second, and then, he burst out laughing. "That was a great joke, Lindsay! I actually thought I heard you say you were engaged to William."

"I did," Lindsay said.

Then, Gerald just became silent all together.

"Gerald," Lindsay began. "I'm sorry. I didn't mean to hurt you. I had to tell you the truth. I care about you too much as a friend to keep this from you."

Gerald continued to be silent.

"Can I call and talk to you later on tonight?" she asked him.

But he just continued to sit there. Not saying a word. Lindsay walked out of the restaurant in disappointment and frustration.

"Man," Anthony leaned over and asked, "are you all right?"

"You know what? I really loved her. I really did!" He tried to hold them back, but the tears of sorrow and remorse came flowing down from his eyes.

Chapter 17

Kayla, Grace, and Skeeter were sitting on the couch watching television. Mrs. Maxey walked downstairs and asked, "Is your father home yet?"

"Nope," Skeeter quickly answered. He was more into watching the television than watching for his dad to come home.

"Hello, everybody!" Rev. Avery Maxey greeted waltzing in the door from outside.

"He is now," Grace responded.

"Our Washington, D.C. expenses are all paid for," Rev. Maxey said to his wife.

"Is Mary staying in a room with us?" she asked.

"Yes."

"What if *we* want to be alone?"

"We'll kick her out!" Rev. Maxey laughed.

"Do we get to go on the D.C. trip, too?" Kayla asked interrupting the laughter.

"No," Rev. Maxey answered.

"Why?" Kayla asked.

"The trip is about a week long, and you'll miss school. And that is a lot of work that you guys will have to make up," Mrs. Maxey answered.

"We are willing to risk it," Skeeter replied.

"No, you guys," Rev. Maxey said in his voice of authority, and silence shot the room.

It was now the evening portion of the day, but it was a special evening because it was the evening of Saint Valentine's Day. All loving couples from around the world would share this wonderful and loving evening together.

But everyone did not have someone to share this day with, and it seemed that all the singles piled up at *Ken's*, including Tyreke. Having been dumped by Eve, he resorted to having dinner alone. He sat at the table eating his dinner. He was not miserable or lonely. He just wanted a friend, preferably a female, to sit with him and enjoy dinner.

Malik walked out of the backroom and over to Tyreke's table. "I see that you are all alone tonight," he said.

"I don't see you with anyone either," Tyreke replied. He had to change the subject. "Anyway, I talked to Sean Powers, the dude that Eve used to date, and he said that he'll room with us on the Washington, D.C. trip. So, now we have three people in a room."

"Four," Malik corrected. "My brother Maurice is staying with us, too." He looked around. "Well, I have to go. I have to do a little bit of inventory."

"All right. I'll catch you later," Tyreke said as Malik walked away. He continued to eat his dinner and listen to the jazz band.

Then, a female sneaked behind Tyreke and whispered, "May I join you?"

Tyreke turned around. "What the... Shawna!"

"Hi!" she greeted, and they shared a friendly hug. "May I sit down?"

"Sure," Tyreke insisted as Shawna sat down in the empty chair next to Tyreke. They started to talk and reminiscence about old times. Tyreke truly believed that Shawna coming to *Ken's* was the Lord's doing. He answered Tyreke's prayers by sending him a friend to dine with – a female.

Chapter 18

Mid-March was just around the corner. Pastor Bruce, Rev. Maxey, and the other office staff were getting the annual church trip to Washington, D.C. organized.

"Pastor," Rev. Maxey said, "we have over a hundred people attending this trip."

"I see that we're probably going to need at least five buses," Pastor Bruce observed.

That evening, Eve and George were toasting to their one-month anniversary in Eve's apartment. The lights were dim, and the music was playing low. It was the perfect mood for a romantic evening.

"This has been a lovely evening," Eve complimented.

"Yes, it has," George replied.

"I wish you were going to D.C. with us," Eve replied.

"I do, too," George said, "but Pastor Bruce announced on Sunday that there are no more rooms available in the hotel. So, no one else can go on the trip unless they room with someone who all ready has a room."

"I would let you stay with me and TJ, but my mother is going to stay with us as well, and she doesn't believe in that *shacking*." Then, a light bulb shone bright in Eve's head. "Wait a minute! I know someone who would be willing to let you stay in a hotel room with him."

Tyreke walked out of his bedroom of his apartment the next morning. As he took a long "wake up" yawn, there was a loud knock on the door. Tyreke walked over to the door and opened it.

"Hi, Tyreke!" Eve greeted. "May I come in?"

"Sure," Tyreke said surprisingly. "Sorry, that I'm not really all that dressed. I wasn't really expecting you so early. Actually, I wasn't expecting you at all. Come in."

Eve walked in with eagerness. "You're going on the trip to Washington, D.C. with the church, right?"

"Yeah. Are you?"

"Of course."

"Why do you ask?" Tyreke began to become suspicious.

"On Sunday, Pastor Bruce announced that there are no more rooms in the hotel we will be staying in, but if any additional people wanted to go, they could room with anyone who all ready had a room. And George..."

Tyreke interrupted her. "Let me guess. You want to know if George can room with me."

"Right. So can he?"

"I would," Tyreke answered, "but I can't."

"Why?" Eve whined.

Oh Lord, not that whining! Tyreke thought. Then, he answered, "It's already four-deep in our room."

"*Our* room?"

"Yeah. Malik, Sean, Malik's little brother, and I are all ready sharing a room. I don't think there will be enough room for George to room with us. I'm sorry."

"Oh. Well, thank you anyway," Eve sadly replied. "I guess I'll talk to you later." She opened the door and walked out. Now, she had to live with the reality that her and George would not be together for a whole week.

Chapter 19

March 18th

Dear Journal,

This week is finally here! The Pearly Gates Baptist Church is finally heading to Washington, D.C. The departure time is 12:01 Monday morning, but it is now 12:30, and we're still at this church waiting on some people to show up. There are five buses out here. The bus in

the front is for Pastor Bruce, the two associate ministers - my dad and Rev. Holiday - , their families (I decided not to ride
that bus though), the deacons, office staff,
and their families. The second bus is for
the teens and youth that requested their
own bus. The other two buses are for the
other members of the church.

I'm chillin' here on the last bus
with my friends and some other adults.
The older adults are sitting in the front of
the bus. I'm sitting sort of in the last row
of the middle portion of the bus. Sean,
Eve's ex, is sitting with me. You know,
he's a pretty nice guy once you get to
know him. I wonder what he saw in Eve,
though?

Anyway, Malik and his brother are
sitting in front of me. Eve and TJ are sitting across from me. Right now, Eve is
looking out the window waving "bye-bye"
and mouthing "I love you" to George.
How pathetic could you get? And that
poor man is on the church stoop doing
the exact same thing to Eve. Cherie and

Kellie are standing next to him outside waving goodbye to people. I wonder what made them want to get up this early to say goodbye to us!

Faith and Tony are sitting together behind me. Tyrone and his boom box are sitting behind Eve and TJ. Pearly Gates most talked about couple, Silk Miller and Denise West, are sitting together way in the back of the bus. Silk and Denise remind me of the famous Shakespearean lovers Romeo and Juliet except for the part that they don't live too far apart and their families don't hate each other, and I don't think they love each other that much to kill themselves (I hope not).

We are staying in the Presidential Hotel. Pastor Bruce, Dad, Mom, Mary, Rev. Holiday, his family, the deacons, the office staff, and their families are staying on the first floor. The teens, youth, and the youth advisors are on the second floor, and the other church members are on the third, fourth, and fifth floor. Sean, Maurice, Malik, Eve, TJ, Faith, Tony, Tyrone, Denise, Silk, and basically everyone on this last bus are on the top floor.

Our rooms are going to be too crunk! Of course, my room is going to be jumpin' because Sean, Malik, Maurice, and me are rooming together. Tony, Tyrone, Silk, his brother Percy, and I guess an old friend from their high school, Reggie Duncan, are staying in a room. Denise, her cousin Teresa West, and her two old college roommates, Holly Robinson and Dee Curry, are staying together. Faith is staying with her best friend Chelsea. This trip is going to be off the chain!

"All aboard!" the bus driver just called out. I guess now we're finally ready to go. He just cranked up the bus. Washington, D.C. here we come!

~Tyreke

The buses finally drove off as George, Kellie, and Cherie waved good-bye. "They're gone. I can't believe it," George replied.

"You're going to miss Eve, aren't you?" Cherie asked pretending to be concerned.

"Most definitely!" George exclaimed.

Just then, a black SUV pulled up to the curb. The driver's side door opened, and Artie got out of the car. He walked over to George and the girls as if he had something up his sleeve.

"Hi, Artie," Kellie greeted trying to break the silence.

Artie stood directly in front of George.

"What do you want?" George asked.

"You know exactly what I want," he responded. "I want my girl back!"

"Well, you are a little too late. She's gone!" George laughed, but it eased into a light chuckle and then, silence.

"Oh... you crackin' jokes! Well, I don't see nothing funny! I'll never forget this! You stole my girl! I promise you, I will get her back! You can count on that!" Artie slid back in the driver's seat and slammed the door. Suddenly, the engine revved up and the black SUV sped off.

"Wow," Kellie observed. "He sounds *really, really* mad!"

Chapter 20

oom 621 was a medium-sized room with two full-sized beds, a color television, a couch that folded out into a bed, a desk with a chair, and a telephone. The bathroom was next to the beds.

The door opened, and Tyreke, Sean, Malik, and Maurice walked in with their bags. Everyone dropped their bags on the floor and relaxed.

"Excuse me, y'all," Sean replied. "I hate to be rude, but I got to hit that toilet!" He ran into the bathroom, turned on the lights and the air ventilation, and closed the door.

"I'm going to see if my parents and Mary are settled in their room," Tyreke said.

"I'll go with you," Malik said. "I have to go back outside to see if I left anything on the bus."

As they walked out of the room, Maurice plopped himself

on one of the beds and turned on the television with the remote control.

Denise and Silk were kissing in front of the door of room 635. Teresa walked out of room 634 and waited until Denise and Silk would notice her standing there, but her patience was wearing thin. She pretended to cough, and Denise and Silk finally stopped kissing to notice that Teresa was standing by them.

"I hate to interrupt you guys," she said, "but Denise, Dee and Holly need your help with something in the room."

"Okay," Denise replied. "Sweetie, I'll see you later." She kissed Silk lightly on the lips. She slowly went to her room and walked in.

Silk noticed that Teresa continued to stare at him. *Should I smile back or should I just go in my room and pretend she isn't there?*

Teresa continued to look and smile at Silk. "You know," Teresa finally said, "Denise is very lucky to have such a good looking man as yourself." She walked into her room and closed door.

Silk stood in front of his room door stunned and confused.

Chapter 21

Malik walked out of the Presidential Hotel. It was a beautiful day, and the sun shone brightly. Malik stood in amazement. *I can't believe I'm actually at our nation's capital.* He walked to the buses that were parked on the curb and over to the bus he came on.

Suddenly, a beautiful woman glided out of the hotel building. Malik could not believe his eyes; she was the most beautiful woman he had ever seen. The young lady passed him with such grace. Malik continued to marvel at her beauty as she boarded the last bus. *Everything is perfect about her*, he thought.

When she got off the bus with her purse, she noticed Malik staring at her. "May I help you?" she wondered.

Then, Malik snapped back into reality. "Um... I was just wondering... um... are you a member of the church?"

"No," she said, "I'm a friend of Denise's. My name is

Dee. And you are?"

"Malik," he answered. "My name is Malik."

"Well, it was very nice to meet you, Malik," Dee said, and she glided back into the Presidential Hotel.

Rev. Maxey, Mrs. Maxey, and Mary were staying in room 104 on the first floor. The elevator bell rang, and the doors slid open. Tyreke walked out of the elevator and over to room 104. As he raised his hand to knock on the door, an attractive young lady opened the door across the hall in room 105. She looked as if she were in her early thirties and at least five feet, eight inches.

"Hi," the young lady greeted.

Tyreke opened his mouth, but the words could not seem to come out. He just gasped and stared. The young lady giggled and walked away.

Just then, the door of room 104 opened, and Rev. Maxey looked at his son as he continued to stare at what was now empty space. "Son," he began, "are you okay?"

"I'm fine, Dad," Tyreke replied. *And so is she!*

Chapter 22

A bright sunrise began the new day. Rev. and Mrs. Maxey were sleeping on the queen-sized bed, and Mary was quietly sleeping on the couch. Mrs. Maxey awakened and smiled. She had something on her mind that she had to do, and she could not wait to put it into action.

Mrs. Maxey arose out of the bed and picked up the phone. She dialed the phone number to her home. The phone continued to ring. Finally, a voice answered, "Hello?"

"Hi! This is Mom! Is this Kayla?

"Yeah. Hi, Mom! How's D.C.?" Kayla asked.

"It's great!" Mrs. Maxey replied. "We really miss you guys."

"We miss you, too. How's Dad, Tyreke, and Mary?"

"They're fine," Mrs. Maxey answered. Then, she smiled and replied, "I just called to wish you a Happy Birthday! Happy

Eighteenth Birthday, sweetheart!"

"Thanks."

"We'll have your party as soon as we get home."

"You better believe it," Kayla laughed.

Malik was sitting on his bed across from Tyreke, who was sitting on his own bed. Maurice was still asleep on the couch. Sean was taking a hot, steamy shower and "trying" to sing. "Ty," Malik began, "you would never believe the girl I met yesterday. The girl was fine! Her name is Dee. She's staying with Denise, Teresa, and Holly."

"Why don't you go to her room and talk to her?" Tyreke asked.

"I don't think I can."

"Why? You scared?"

"Um... yeah. I'm afraid I all ready made a fool of myself," Malik confessed.

Tyreke began to tell his story. "Well, the girl I met has something mystifying about her. She is beautiful. Man, she's just drop-dead gorgeous!"

"What's her name?" Malik asked.

"I don't know," Tyreke replied. "When I saw her, I was speechless. All I know is she is staying across the hall from my parents."

"Maybe I should go talk to Dee," Malik concluded.

"And maybe I'll go see my mysterious woman," Tyreke smiled.

Silk opened his eyes and felt the bright sun shining on his face. While yawning, he reached under his pillow and felt a piece of paper folded down. He pulled it out and opened it.

Dear Silk,

Hi! I want to see you. Meet me at La Mamba today at noon.
~Teresa

P.S. Don't tell Denise that you're meeting me. I don't want her all up in my business.

Chapter 23

ilk slipped on a pair of clothes that were lying beside his bed. Then, he slid on his shoes. *Should I really be doing this? I mean, I love Denise, but Teresa has something about her.*

Percy, Tony, Tyrone, and Reggie were still sleeping. The room was a mess as if they had a wild party.

Silk tried to slip out of the room quietly, but Tony lifted his head and saw Silk trying to leave. "Where are you going?" he asked.

"Out," Silk replied.

"With Denise?"

"Yeah. Whatever," he lied.

"Oh. Have fun," Tony said as Silk walked out the door. Then, he dropped his head and drifted back to sleep.

Holly and Dee were sitting on the couch watching television while Denise was in the bathroom washing her hair. There was a knock on the door. Dee got up and opened the door. Malik was standing at the door as nervous as can be. "Hi," he said.

"Hey, Malik," Dee smiled.

"Are you busy?" Malik asked.

"No. Not really. Why?"

Malik was shaking, but he had to do this. "Maybe we could go out to lunch and talk," Malik suggested.

"Okay. Where do you want to go?"

"I heard about a Mexican place around the corner from the hotel. We could go there," Malik said.

"That's fine with me," Dee replied. Then, she turned to Holly. "I'll be back a little later."

"Okay," Holly responded as Malik and Dee walked out and closed the door.

Tyreke walked into the lobby area of the Presidential Hotel. He sat on the couch and picked up the newspaper to read it.

Out of nowhere, the beautiful, mysterious woman that

Tyreke saw yesterday appeared in front of him when he looked up from reading. "Hi," she said.

Again, Tyreke became speechless. *No*, he thought. *I'm not doing this again!* He finally caught his breath and uttered, "Hello."

"Are you finished with the paper? I'd like to read the sports section?" she asked.

"Before I give you what you want," Tyreke replied trying to be charming, "you have to give me what I want."

"And what do you want?"

"For starters, what's your name?" Tyreke cleverly asked.

"My name is Tamera. Is that all?"

"How about we have dinner tonight so I can get to know you better?"

"Fine," Tamera replied. "Now, can I have the sports section?"

"Sure," Tyreke smiled handing Tamera the paper. *I am the man!*

La Mamba was an outside, Mexican restaurant with very friendly service. Silk and Teresa were sitting at a small table eating. "So, what was so important that you had to hide a little note under my pillow and keep it a secret from my girl?" Silk asked.

"Well," Teresa grinned, "I actually have more of a confession to make. Silk, I understand the fact that you are dating my cousin, but I can't help but feel a deep desire to have you for myself."

"That's it?"

"Pretty much."

"Well," Silk began to grin, "I have a confession as well. I feel the same way."

"You do? I don't believe it."

"Oh, yeah. Let me show you." Silk leaned over and started to kiss Teresa.

Malik and Dee walked into *La Mamba*. "It's kind of weird to go into another restaurant besides my own," Malik said.

"You own a restaurant?" Dee asked.

"Yeah," Malik said. "The name of my restaurant is *Ken's*. I named it after my grandfather."

"That's nice," Dee replied. She began to observe the place to find somewhere to sit, but something distracted her. "Malik! Look!"

Malik turned around, and he saw Teresa and Silk sharing a passionate kiss.

Chapter 24

ve was sitting at the desk in her room talking on the phone with George. TJ was snoring like his father on the bed. "So, how is everything back home?" Eve asked.

"It's okay," George answered on the other line. "But we have a little situation with Artie."

"What's up?" Eve seemed concerned.

"Well, after you guys left the church, Artie pulled up, and he told me that he wanted *you* back. Well, I didn't really let that phase me, but for the past few days when I run into him, he gives me these hard, cold stares."

"Maybe I'll just talk to him when we get back," Eve suggested.

"No," George requested. "It'll just stir up more trouble."

There was a knock on the door. "I got to go," she said. "I'll talk to you later."

"Okay. I love you!" George exclaimed.

"Love you, too!" Eve smiled as she hung up the phone. She stood up and opened the door.

Tyreke was standing at the door. "Hey," he greeted. "I just came by to see if little man wanted to do something right now, but I see he's sleep."

"Ty," Eve said, "if you're not doing anything later on this evening, maybe me, you, Teej, and my mother could go out to dinner somewhere."

"I'd love to, but I have a date tonight," Tyreke smiled mischievously.

"Date? Ha! What *hoochie* is it this time?"

"First of all, she's not a hoochie. She's a lovely young lady with a great personality, unlike some people. Second, I don't see how any of this is any of your business."

"I'm sorry," Eve apologized. "I didn't mean to come at you like that."

"Apology accepted," Tyreke replied. "I'll see you later."

As Tyreke walked away, Eve closed the door and sighed.

The Presidential Hotel had an Olympic-sized pool with a beautiful aqua color. Tyrone, Reggie, Holly, Denise, and Percy were in the pool swimming and dunking each other. Tony and Faith were sitting at a table on the pool deck.

Malik and Dee walked on the deck and walked to the table where Faith and Tony were. "Hey, guys!" Tony and Faith greeted.

"You two will never believe what we saw," Dee said.

"What?" Tony curiously asked.

"We saw Silk at *La Mamba*," Malik said.

"So?" Faith was curious to know what Dee was talking about.

"He was there with Teresa," Dee concluded.

"And let's just say *her* gum ended up in *his* mouth," Malik added.

Tony and Faith gasped.

"And speaking of the devils," Dee said as Teresa and Silk walked over to the pool.

Denise swam to the edge of the pool. "Hey, you two," she greeted. "Where have you guys been?"

Silk and Teresa looked at each other trying to figure out what to say. "Um…. um… I was making some phone calls," Teresa said.

"I took a walk around. Saw some sights." And then, he added, "I bought you something."

"Awww, that was sweet," Denise smiled. She met up with Silk, and they kissed.

Faith, Tony, Dee, and Malik looked at them from the deck. "How could he kiss Denise after he just finished making out with Teresa?" Malik wondered.

"What a dog!" Dee exclaimed.

Chapter 25

That evening, Malik, Maurice, and Sean were sitting in the room playing Spades. There was a knock on the door. "Come in!" Malik called.

The door opened, and Tony walked in and greeted, "What's up, fellas!"

"What's up?" Sean asked slamming his ace of diamonds on the table.

"I just wanted to let you guys know that we are going to have another one of our parties in our room tonight," Tony said. "You are welcome to come."

"All right!" Maurice shouted.

"We'll be there," Malik replied.

"All right," Tony smiled.

Suddenly, Tyreke walked out of the bathroom in a black suit and a green shirt. "Cous, you look good, man! Where are you off to?"

"I have a date with Tamera," Tyreke bragged.

"Way to go!" Malik congratulated.

"Maybe after your date you can bring her by the little get together in our room," Tony suggested.

"Okay, I will!" Tyreke replied fixing his tie.

"Cool," Tony responded. "Well, see y'all later." He walked out and closed the door behind him.

Madame Wilson was a petite restaurant on the corner of Liberty Avenue and Clinton Road. It was not very crowded, and the atmosphere of the restaurant was so quiet a pin drop could be heard. There was a calm and still presence that made *Madame Wilson* so popular.

Tyreke and Tamera were sitting at a table laughing and enjoying each other's company. "I'm having a great time tonight," Tyreke said. "I love being with you. I feel--"

"Tyreke!" Tamera interrupted. "I have to say something! I like you a lot, but I'm all ready in a serious relationship."

"What?" Tyreke was confused. He felt like his heart had literally been ripped from his chest and stuffed down his throat.

"Tyreke, I'm sorry. I know I should've told you sooner. I hope you can find it in your heart to forgive me," she apologized.

Tyreke sat back in his seat in disgust, disbelief, and disappointment.

The party was jumping in room 635. Everyone was having a good time – some more than others.

Silk and Denise were dancing together. "I'm having a good time!" Denise replied. "How about you?"

Silk did not respond. He turned around and noticed that Teresa was sitting on the couch bobbing her head to the music.

"Hello? Silk?" Silk finally noticed that Denise was talking to him. "Did you hear me? Are you having a good time?"

"Yeah, yeah," Silk replied not really paying attention to her. "Baby, let me go get us some punch."

"Okay," Denise said as Silk slid away. *That's funny. I don't remember asking for a drink*, she thought.

Silk walked over to Teresa trying to be unnoticeable to Denise.

"Hi," Teresa smiled.

"What's up! You want to go and talk in the back room?" Silk asked.

"Sure," Teresa said as her and Silk walked to the back room.

Denise was standing at the same spot by herself for about ten minutes now. Holly, Dee, and Malik walked over to her. "Dang, girl! You've been dancing by yourself for quite a while now," Malik observed.

"Where's Silk?" Holly asked.

"He said he was going to get us both some punch," Denise replied.

"I think that maybe you should go and look for him," Dee suggested. She wanted Silk and Teresa to be busted.

"I'll be back," Denise said walking away. First, she checked the punch table; he was not there. Then, she looked for him at the snack table; he was not there either.

Denise walked over to the couch and saw Tyreke sitting there alone. "Hey," she greeted. "Have you seen Silk?"

"No," Tyreke replied sadly.

"What's the matter?" Denise asked with concern.

"I don't want to talk about it right now."

"Oh. Okay," she said. Then, Denise peeked her head in the back room, and to her surprise, she saw her cousin and her boyfriend sitting on the bed... kissing.

Chapter 26

March 24th

Dear Journal,

    We have finally pulled off from the Presidential Hotel to head back home. The bus I'm on is very quiet right now. No one is saying a word.

    Sean is asleep beside me, and Maurice decided to ride on the first bus and talk with my sister. Is something going on between Maurice and Mary? I guess we'll see when we get home.

It seems as if Malik has made a new "friend". He and Dee are sitting right in front of me and Sean laughing and talking. It looks like they hit it off very well; unlike me and Tamera. I still can't believe she has a boyfriend and how she led me on like that. I am really, really devastated.

Eve and TJ are sitting across from me. TJ is looking at a picture book; Eve is listening to her CD player. (And probably thinking about George, too.)

But it is really quiet on the back of the bus, which is a real surprise. Faith and Tony have their heads together sleeping. I'm very surprised that Silk and Denise aren't all up on each other. I wonder what's up with them. All I know is after Denise checked that back room, the sad and disappointed expression on her face hasn't left. I just pray that we get home safely.

~Tyreke

Tyreke put his journal and pen back in his book bag. Eve pulled off her headphones and leaned over to Tyreke. "May I hold your cell phone?" she asked Tyreke. "I need to call George to see if he's at the church or not."

"I'm sorry, Eve. My phone's not charged up," he said.

Eve shrugged and put her headphones back on her head.

Denise and Silk sat quietly in their seats. Denise sat in disgust because she knew her boyfriend was cheating on her with her cousin. She did not say anything about it because neither Silk nor Teresa knew that Denise saw them making out in the backroom in Washington, D.C. in room 635 at 10:05 PM.

Silk noticed how quiet Denise was. *I feel so bad. I shouldn't be treating her like this. But I can't help the way that I feel,* he thought. "Is there something wrong?"

"No," Denise replied bluntly. "Nothing's wrong. Nothing at all."

George was waiting on the steps of the Pearly Gates Baptist Church for the buses from Washington, D.C. that cool evening. He was eager and excited to see Eve. It had been a whole week since he had seen his girlfriend. George and Eve had a serious relationship for about two months now. George held his head down and prayed that the buses would return safely from D.C.

Then, he heard stomps coming towards him. George lifted his head, and he recognized the boots, clothes, and the figure. He stared into the figure's cold eyes. "Artie," George finally spoke, "what are you doing here?"

"I'm here to see if everyone got back home safely," Artie replied.

"And to see Eve," George snapped.

"Man, what's your beef?" Artie shouted.

"No! What's yours?"

"I believe I asked you first," Artie said.

"Believe it or not, I have none with you. You're the one starting all of this mess with me." Then, he asked, "Why?"

"You stole my woman!" Artie shouted.

"She was never your woman to begin with!"

"She would've been in time," he replied. "It's all my fault. I should've never introduced you two!"

"Well, I guess it's a little too late for that now. Isn't it?" George responded.

Artie lifted his hand as if he was going to strike George in the face and cried, "Boy, I'll knock---"

Then, the five buses pulled up in the parking lot. George and Artie turned around and saw them. "You lucky," he said and walked away.

George sighed in relief. He looked for Artie, but he was nowhere to be found. Vanished. Then, George looked up and saw Eve wave and smile at him from the bus in the back.

Chapter 27

April flew by quickly. Everything seemed to have gone back to normal. Tyreke was handling things at *The Boss Chronicle* while Mr. Boss was still on his safari with his wife. Eve and George had a great relationship even though Artie continued to badger them and complicate their lives. Lindsay and William were still happily engaged. Malik and Dee had a meaningful relationship, even though it was kind of on and off. Even things between Denise and Silk were back to normal; it was like nothing happened back in Washington, D.C.

It was a warm and sunny day in early May, and things were running smoothly at *The Boss Chronicle* office. It had been three months since that little "confrontation" with Mr. Boss's son, Aaron.

Tyreke walked into the building and to his desk with a smile on his face. Francis walked over to him with a hot and steamy cup of coffee and placed it on Tyreke's desk. "Good morning," she greeted.

"Hey! What's up?"

"You had a call from Mr. Boss. He's back in town," Francis reported.

"I wonder if Aaron has talked to him," Tyreke replied.

"Let's hope not," Francis said smiling as she walked back to her desk.

Bing! The sound of the elevator rung in everyone's ears as the elevator doors opened. To everyone's surprise, Mr. Boss and Aaron walked in. They had on identical suits, which were black with thin, white stripes in their jackets and slacks.

With excitement, everyone, including Francis, crowded around them, except Tyreke. *This could only lead to bad news,* he thought as he started doing work on his computer as if nothing was going on.

Everyone was clamoring around Mr. Boss and his son as if they were movie stars. "Good morning, all!" Mr. Boss began in an exuberant voice. "As you can all see, I am back! My wife and I had a very nice time in South Africa! We didn't expect to stay down there as long as we did. We helped a lot of people, and we enjoyed doing it. That's why my wife and I have decided to move down to South Africa and continue to do what we can to help out."

The staff began to all talk at once. "Oh no!"

"Why?"

"We will surely miss you!"

Then, a voice spoke out. "Who will run *The Boss Chronicle*?" It was the voice of Francis; she seemed to be the voice of reason.

"I'm glad you asked," Mr. Boss grinned, and then he looked at his shoulder. "I am giving the ownership of *The Boss Chronicle* to my beloved son, Aaron."

Everyone clapped in admiration for Aaron, except Francis who turned away and walked over to Tyreke, who was still working and ignoring the "praise party."

"Thank you! Thank you! I will try to do a good of a job as my father," Aaron smiled.

What a fake! Tyreke thought.

Then, Aaron continued, "I would like to give a special thanks to Tyreke, who did an excellent job running the place during my father's absence!"

Everyone turned and clapped towards Tyreke. What could he do? He had done a good job while Mr. Boss was away. The only thing he could do was smile.

"I am now going to let my son take over from here," Mr. Boss smiled and walked into the opened doors of the elevator.

As the sliding doors closed, the crowd began to scatter and sit at their workplaces. "Wow. Wasn't that exciting?" Francis asked Tyreke in a sarcastic tone.

"Very," he replied with the same bit of sarcasm.

Aaron, with his hands in his pants pockets, walked over to Francis and Tyreke. "Hello, you two," he greeted with a sly grin.

"Nice to see you again," Tyreke responded.

"You didn't seem this happy to see me three months ago," Aaron replied. "You two ought to be nice to me now that I OWN *The Boss Chronicle*."

"Congratulations," Francis said trying to be nice.

"So, what is your first duty as the new owner?" Tyreke pretended to be interested.

"My first duty is to appoint myself editor," Aaron said.

"Editor?" Francis and Tyreke both shouted.

Then, Francis asked, "But what about Tyreke? What will he do?"

"You and Mr. Maxey will *share* the position of assistant editor."

"But..."

"I have made my decision," Aaron demanded. "Now get to work!" He walked away.

Francis began to fuss. "I can't believe he---"

"Francis, save it," Tyreke said. "What's done is done." And he continued to work on his computer.

Fantasy was a usually crowded nightclub. Everyone always came to have a good time and usually DANCE. That night, the club was crowded from the bar to the tables to the dance floor.

Gerald and Anthony were sitting at a table. Gerald was eating his nachos and super cheesy cheese while Anthony was grubbing on the free salted peanuts on the basket on the table. "Are you just going to eat those peanuts?" Gerald asked.

"Yep!"

"Why?"

"Because they're free!" Anthony replied.

"You know they make those peanuts free and extra salty to make you buy a drink," Gerald informed his ignorant friend.

"Now, that I think about it, I am kind of thirsty," Anthony said. Then, he coughed as if he was choking and called out, "WATER! WATER!" As he looked around for a waitress, he saw something he could not believe.

Anthony tapped Gerald on his shoulder and said, "Look." He pointed to the dance floor.

Gerald gasped. "I can't believe it!" he exclaimed as he and Anthony were looking at William dancing very closely to another woman that was *not* Lindsay.

Lindsay was sitting at the table in the kitchen in her mother's house. Mrs. Carney walked into the kitchen from the living and asked, "What are you up to?"

"Wedding stuff," Lindsay replied. "I've all ready sold the apartment and moved into William's condo. I can't wait until we finally tie the knot! I am so excited!"

Chapter 28

Tyreke did not walk in the *Boss Chronicle* the next morning with the usual happy expression on his face. *Why?* He'd often asked himself that. *Why me?* Tyreke placed his travel bag at his desk, sat in his chair, powered up his computer, and prepared for work.

Aaron walked out of what was now his office and over to Tyreke's desk. "Can I help you?" Tyreke asked sarcastically.

"Mr. Maxey, can I see you in my office please?" Aaron asked in a surprisingly nice way.

Offended by his phoniness, Tyreke followed Aaron into his office and closed the door. "Have a seat," Aaron said as he sat in his father's leather chair.

"I'd rather stand," Tyreke stubbornly responded.

"Fine. Have it your way."

"Aaron, what do you want with me?" Tyreke impatiently

asked.

"Mr. Maxey, I have treated you with respect. Now, how about you do the same for me. Understand?"

"Yes, your Excellency!" Tyreke rolled his eyes.

"Mr. Maxey, I have called you in here because I have an assignment for you. Here," Aaron said handing Tyreke a sheet of paper with a list of names on it.

Tyreke looked over and quickly scanned the names. "What's this?"

"Have you heard of a writer by the name of Al Barber?" Aaron asked. That question did not seem to have anything to do with the paper he handed Tyreke or Tyreke's question.

"Al Barber? Yeah!" Tyreke seemed to be interested. "What about him?"

"Well, I have convinced him to come write for *The Boss Chronicle*," Aaron smiled.

"That's great! But what does that have to do with me and this piece of paper?"

"Al is demanding a huge salary," Aaron admitted. "So, that is resulting in either huge pay cuts or the laying off of some employees."

"And..."

"I'm sure you guys need every penny you can get," Aaron snickered. "So, I've decided to lay-off some people."

Tyreke surveyed the list, and then he recognized a familiar name. "You have Francis's name on here!" Tyreke shouted.

"It was a tough decision between you and Francis," Aaron replied. "Even tougher since you *repulse* me, but next to me, you're the next best writer we have around here."

"So, you expect me to tell all of these people including a

good friend of mine that we don't need them anymore?" Tyreke asked.

"Exactly."

"Why can't you do it?" Tyreke challenged. "You are *the boss!*"

"It's not in my job description," Aaron responded.

"It's not in mine, either!" Tyreke shouted.

"It is now! So as the editor and owner of this newspaper, I *command* you to do your job, which is right now to deliver the news to the employees on that list."

Tyreke walked out of the office without looking back. Then, Francis walked up to him with a smile on her face and greeted, "Hi, Ty!"

Gerald was talking to Anthony on the phone. "So, are you going to tell Lindsay what we saw last night?"

"I can't," Gerald replied.

"And why not? William is a dirty scumbag! He should be exposed! Lindsay's our friend."

"Like my mama always said," Gerald stated, "whatever is done in the darkness will eventually come out in the light."

Lindsay walked out of the grocery store with milk, eggs, and bread in a plastic bag. She walked over to the jeep and opened the door to place the bag down in the seat. After she closed the door, she turned around and saw William walking out of the grocery store. *I didn't see him while I was in there,* Lindsay wondered.

Then, she gasped. A young, Puerto Rican woman walked out of the grocery store, slipped her hand in his, and lightly kissed him on the lips. In rage, Lindsay stormed over to William and his female companion.

Shocked, William responded, "LINDSAY!"

"Honey, who is this?" the Puerto Rican woman asked.

"I'm his fiancé," Lindsay replied. "Or shall I say ex-fiancé." And she pulled the ring off her finger and dropped it on the road.

"What was that all about?" the Puerto Rican asked as if she did not hear the conversation at all.

"Let's go," William said as he picked up the engagement ring off the road and walked to his car pulling her along.

Crying, but making sure he did not see her, Lindsay walked to her jeep.

Chapter 29

*I*t had been several months since Mary's sorority moved into Tyreke's house. The sorority was known to host a few wild parties, but they also did a lot of work in the community and for the environment.

Mary decided to take a break this weekend. She sat on her bed reading a fictional novel. Then, there was a knock on the door. "Come in!"

The door opened, and her sorority sister walked in. "Here's your mail," she said.

"Just throw it on the bed," Mary replied.

Mary's sorority sister threw the mail on her bed, and she walked out the room and closed the door. Mary folded down the edge of the page she stopped on and closed the book. She crawled to the mail that was now splattered on her bed and went through her mail: junk, junk, junk.

Then, Mary pulled out an en envelope under the junk mail. *What's this?* she wondered. She saw that the return address was from Jenkins Medical School. Mary applied to Jenkins last year, but she was put on the waiting list. *I wonder what this could be.*

Mary ripped the envelope open. She pulled out the letter skimmed through it. Then, she dropped the letter and began to jump up and down on her bed screaming from the top of her lungs. "I've been accepted!" she screamed. "I'm going to be going to Jenkins Medical School in Savannah, Georgia in the fall!"

Kayla, Skeeter, and Grace went to Freeman High School. Grace was a freshman; Skeeter was a junior. Kayla was a senior, who had the potential of being valedictorian of her class. Kayla could get into any college she wanted to with her straight A status and a 2180 SAT score.

It was three o'clock that afternoon, and Mrs. Maxey was sitting on the couch waiting for her three babies to come home. Then, the three youngest Maxey children walked in the front door. "Hi, Mom!" they greeted.

"Hey, guys," Mrs. Maxey smiled. "How was school today?"

"Fine," Grace replied. She kissed her mom on the cheek and walked into the kitchen.

"Skeeter?"

"It was all right," he responded. He kissed his mother on the cheek and ran upstairs to his bedroom.

"Did I get any mail?" Kayla asked.

"As a matter of fact," Mrs. Maxey said picking up an envelope, "you did." She handed Kayla the envelope.

"This is from Athens University!" Kayla cried.

"Open it!" Mrs. Maxey was as excited as her daughter was.

Kayla ripped the envelope open and read it. Mumbling. And then she shouted, "I got in! I'm going to Athens University in the fall!"

Kayla hugged Mrs. Maxey, and they both jumped up and down with joy and excitement.

Chapter 30

The Pearly Gates Baptist Church annually had an appreciation banquet for Pastor Bruce. Pastor Bruce would always go out of his way to do whatever he could for the church; therefore, this banquet was to show him how much they appreciated him. The banquet would be held in the ballroom of the Hallway Hotel.

It was now Sunday afternoon, and the church services for Pearly Gates Baptist Church ended. The door opened, and everyone walked outside and prepared to go home.

Tyreke, Tyrone, Tony, Faith, George, Silk, Denise, and Robin Allen walked down the stairs and scattered around in their little group. "So, is anyone going to the Pastor Appreciation Banquet?" Denise asked in her perky voice while being hugged and cuddled by Silk.

Everyone, except Tyrone, mumbled a yes.

"What are you wearing?" Tony asked Faith.

"I am going to buy a gold gown with some Cinderella-like shoes," she replied.

"What about you?" Silk asked Denise.

"I don't know," Denise replied. "but me, Holly, and Teresa are going to the mall today."

Teresa, Silk thought. "Oh," he finally said.

Denise turned to Robin. "Robin, would you like to come with us?"

"Sure. But I don't know if I'm going to the banquet," she said. And, then she flashed those pearly whites.

Tyreke noticed her beautiful smile. Robin Allen was a business consultant in Atlanta. When she came to visit her family, Robin always came to attend her home church.

"Why?" Tyreke asked.

"Why what?" Robin asked back.

"Why aren't you going to the banquet?" Tyreke specified what he meant by his question.

"Those tickets are kind of *steep*," she admitted. "$35!"

"But you are a business consultant. You're making the big money!"

"Well, for a business consultant on a budget, $35 is kind of steep."

"But that's only if you come by yourself," Tyreke explained. "It's $40 for couples."

"But I don't have anyone to go with." She smiled again. That smile! It really got to him.

"Maybe we could go," Tyreke suggested, "together."

Tony, Tyrone, Faith, George, Silk, and Denise gasped.

"Um..." Robin smiled again. "Sure. I'd love to." Then,

she addressed Denise, "I'll see you later."

"Call me," Denise called as Robin walked away.

Tony, Tyrone, George, and Silk started hollering. "BIG DOG! PLAYA, PLAYA!"

"Man, y'all need to quit!" Tyreke laughed. "So, George, are you and Eve going to *try* and make a grand appearance?"

"Eve's coming down with the flu," George said. "Looks like I'll be riding solo that night. So, Tyrone, will you be needing a ride?"

"Nope," Tyrone responded. "I'm not going to the banquet."

"Why? You couldn't find a date?" Denise joked.

"Ha, ha," Tyrone sarcastically responded. "At least the person I'm with is not two-timing me for my cousin like Silk is with you!" Then, he realized what he just did. "Oops."

Tyreke, George, Faith, and Tony look at each other and walked away. Silk gave Tyrone a hard, cold stare. Denise was so hurt. She could not look Silk in his face. "My bad," Tyrone apologized, and he followed behind Tyreke, Tony, Faith, and George.

"So," Denise finally began to speak, "you are seeing Teresa behind my back. Let me ask you one thing. Why?"

"Well… see…" Silk began to stutter. He remembered the first time he saw Teresa. He was so stunned by her beauty.

"No answer. Go figure."

"Let me explain, baby---"

"Save it! It's over! We're through!" Denise shouted. She slowly walked off the church steps without looking back.

Chapter 31

"Here, Mommy!" TJ said giving Eve a cup of orange juice.

"Thank you, baby," his mother smiled and sipped the orange juice.

Then, the telephone rang. "I'll get it!" TJ said as he ran to the telephone. He looked on the Caller I.D. "It's Artie."

"Don't answer it," Eve replied, and she laid her head down. "I don't have time for that."

Artie hung up the phone. *I guess she's not home*, he thought. He was so love sick over Eve. He still remembered the day that he introduced his so-called friend George to his true love. He regretted he did that ever since he found out that "the back stabber" and Eve were dating.

Deep in his thoughts, he heard a knock on the door. Artie lived in a small apartment with his grandmother and his roommate who hardly came home until the morning.

Artie raised and opened the door. To his surprise, Denise was standing at the door with tears in her eyes. "Denise?"

"May I come in?" she asked in her pitiful voice.

"Sure. Come in!" he replied as she walked in, and he closed the door. "Sit down." Denise sat down on the couch, and Artie sat right beside her. "What's the matter?"

Then, she bawled. During the crying, the snuffles, and the tears, Denise broke down and told Artie everything: what happened in D.C. to what happened this afternoon after church.

"Oh." He did not know what to say, but he did know how she felt. She was stabbed in the back by her cousin and her now ex-boyfriend just as he was stabbed in the back by George and Eve. He wanted to sort-of change the subject. "Are you still going to the banquet?"

Denise jumped up. "Yeah! I paid all that money to order my dress and someone is going to see me in it!"

Artie got an idea. "Well, I don't have a date either," Artie started, but Denise stopped him.

"I don't really want a date," she confessed.

"Well, how about an escort?"

"Well... okay. That sounds fine." They smiled at each

other and hugged. The rays of the sun shone bright on their happy faces.

"She knows."

"Oh. Well… it was only a matter of time," Teresa said on the other line.

"So, it looks like we can make our relationship public now," Silk smiled. "Do you have your dress?"

"Of course. Do you have your tux?"

"Most def! I can't wait to see you!"

"Love you!" Teresa smiled.

"Love you, too!" Silk hung up the phone and smiled. But then, the smile disappeared. He began to think about Denise.

Chapter 32

The Hallway Hotel was an extravagant place: fancy and full of culture. The Pastor Appreciation Banquet Committee came that Friday afternoon and decorated the ballroom of the Hallway Hotel. The theme for the evening was "A Great Man of God." The colors were red, silver, and white--- the colors of Pastor Bruce's alma mater. The room was decorated with red, silver, and white balloons, streamers, and cloths on the tables. The night was going to be excellent!

Especially for Tyreke since he had a date with Robin Allen. She was a very beautiful and intelligent woman who was also a Christian, which was the best thing. The only problem that presented itself would be the long distance. *Would she really be interested in me?* he wondered as he put his blue cummerbund around his waist. He adjusted his blue bow tie and slid on his jacket. Tyreke looked at his watch. "Time to go pick up my date."

He opened the door and walked out of the apartment.

The ballroom was beginning to pile up with people. Pastor Bruce was sitting at the head table with his date. Also at the head table were Rev. and Mrs. Maxey, the other associate minister, his wife, the deacons, and their wives. People came up to Pastor Bruce shaking his hand to congratulate and thank him.

At a table close to the door, Faith and Tony were sitting alone. "Where is everyone else?" Faith asked.

"I don't know," Tony replied, "but if no one shows up in about five minutes, we're leaving."

"We don't have to wait for five minutes," Faith responded. "We can leave now."

As they were about to rise up out of their seats, Tyreke and Robin walked in. Robin had on a sparkling, blue dress with blue pumps. "Girl, you are shiny!" Tony jived.

"Shut up, Tony!" Faith snapped. "Robin, you look wonderful."

"She sure does!" Tyreke complimented looking at Robin and smiling.

"Thank you," Robin smiled as she and Tyreke sat across from Faith and Tony.

"Where's everyone else?" Tyreke asked.

"Let's not go down that road again," Tony replied.

Then, Silk and Teresa walked in. Shocked, Tyreke, Robin, Tony, and Faith looked at Teresa and Silk as they sat down beside

Robin and Tyreke.

Smiling, Teresa greeted, "Hi, guys!"

No one knew what to say. Everyone knew what went down between Silk, Denise, and Teresa. To break the silence at the table, Faith replied, "Teresa, you look very nice tonight!"

"Thank you," she said. "You do, too."

The program began to start. George was standing at the door where no one could see him when the Master of Ceremonies stood at the podium and introduced the man of the hour.

"Why are you standing here?" a female voice asked from behind George.

Startled, George turned around to notice that Holly was standing behind him. "Why are you just standing here?" she repeated.

"Just waiting on the right time to make my grand entrance," he lied.

"So, basically you don't want to walk in alone," Holly concluded. She could tell George was lying.

"Oh, I guess you figured me out."

"Would you like to escort me to my seat?" Holly asked.

"It would be my honor." Holly put her arm in his, and they walked into the room and sat at the table across from the rest of the group. Holly and George exchanged quiet "hellos."

"And now we will have a solo by Jack Brown." The MC sat down, and the soloist stood at the podium and started to sing a tribute to Pastor Bruce.

As Mr. Brown was singing, Faith, Tony, Silk, Teresa, Tyreke, and Robin turned around. To their surprise, Denise and Artie were arm-in-arm standing at the door. "Why is everyone staring?" she asked.

"Because they are adjusting their eyes to how beautiful you look tonight," Artie smiled.

"That was sweet," Denise said. She kissed Artie on the cheek. Then, Denise and Artie walked to the table across from them and sat next to Holly and George. Silk looked over at the other table and exchanged glanced with Denise.

She's beautiful! he thought. By the time, Silk could finish his complete thought, Mr. Brown finished his solo and sat down in his seat. Applauds were everywhere.

Tyreke and Robin walked to Robin's door laughing. "I had a great time!" Robin replied.

"I'm glad you did," Tyreke responded. He looked at his watch, and it read 1:35 AM. "When are you heading back to ATL?"

"After church on Sunday."

"Well, good night," Tyreke said.

"Good night," Robin smiled. *That smile!* Tyreke had to do something to make this night memorable. Tyreke puckered his lips and aimed for Robin's beautiful, thin lips, but his lips landed on her soft cheek.

"Why, thank you," she smiled again.

"You're welcome," Tyreke said as he turned around and walked to his car. Robin walked into her house. Tyreke got in his car and turned on the engine. He drove off thinking that he would never forget this night as long as he lived.

Chapter 33

The weekend flew by quickly. Too quickly for Tyreke. Tyreke continued to reminiscence about the fun he had at the Pastor's Appreciation Banquet and how much he enjoyed being in the company of the lovely Robin Allen.

The only thing Tyreke hated about Sundays was Mondays. He hated going to work Mondays through Fridays. Tyreke used to have a passion for working at *The Boss Chronicle*, but now he could not wait until the day he either got fired or the day he would quit.

That Monday morning, Tyreke walked into *The Boss Chronicle* expecting the usual. He would work with a nonchalant attitude, and Aaron Boss would always find a reason to criticize him in a harmful and negative way.

But things were different this morning. Tyreke sat at his desk and turned on his computer. Aaron's office door opened, but it was not Aaron who walked out. It was a female; it was Aaron's sister, Amy. *Thank God!* Tyreke thought. *What a relief!*

Amy walked to his desk. "Hi, Tyreke!" she greeted.

"What's up!" he smiled. He has not smiled in a long time since Aaron came to power at the office. "What are you doing here? Where's Aaron?"

"Surprisingly, he's on his honeymoon with his new wife. He got married last weekend."

"Aaron? Got married? What desperate girl would want to marry him?"

"That's what I said," Amy laughed. "I'm taking over until he gets back. Believe me, this will be a stress-free week."

Mrs. Maxey was finished cleaning the house. She had been cleaning up since sunrise. The Maxey family was expecting company this afternoon.

The front door opened, and Kayla, Grace, and Skeeter rushed in. "Hi, kids!" Mrs. Maxey greeted.

"Is he here yet?" Grace asked.

"No," she replied. "Not yet."

"This is so exciting!" Kayla exclaimed. "We are going to be hosting a foreign exchange student."

"Finally, another guy besides Dad in the house," Skeeter replied.

"Where's he from?" Kayla asked. She was always a curious person.

"He's from England," Mrs. Maxey answered. "You guys go on ahead and wash up. We're going to have dinner as soon as Ben gets here."

Obediently, Kayla, Skeeter, and Grace ran upstairs.

Rev. Maxey walked in from the kitchen. "Can we eat now?" he whined. "That food in there smells *so* good, and I am *so* hungry!"

"No," Mrs. Maxey said. "You have to wait until Ben gets here."

Rev. Maxey walked over to his wife and planted a light kiss on her cheek. "Please?" he protested.

"Go ahead, but don't let the kids see you," she smiled.

"Thanks!" Rev. Maxey ran to the kitchen joyfully.

The doorbell chimed. Mrs. Maxey walked to the door and opened it. A tall, light-skinned, chubby young man wearing a navy blue uniform was standing at the door. "Is this the Maxey residence?" he asked with a light British accent.

"Yes," Mrs. Maxey replied. "Are you Ben Lorry?"

"Yes, I am," Ben said. He walked in with his suitcases. "First, I must say that I am thankful that you have opened up your home to me." He seemed sincere.

"Son," Mrs. Maxey was almost in tears, "welcome to the family." She gave Ben a warm hug like mother to son.

Chapter 34

By the time Tyreke was starting to enjoy work again, the stress-free week was over. When Aaron walked in Monday morning, Amy was not there. The shadow of nonchalance appeared across Tyreke's face as soon as Aaron approached his desk that morning. "Good morning, Mr. Maxey," Aaron greeted with his sly grin.

Tyreke had to admit Aaron looked a little different since the last time he saw him. "Hello, Aaron," Tyreke replied. "How was your honeymoon?"

"Great! Isn't it great to have someone to love and be with?" Then, Aaron snickered. "Oops, I forgot. You aren't with anyone right now, are you?" He laughed all the way to his office.

Tyreke sat in his chair. No comment came from his lips. He was tired of being verbally abused by Aaron all the time. He was tired of being treated with injustice and unfairness. He was not going to just sit on his behind and continue to be treated like a nobody.

Just as he stood up, the telephone rang. "Hello!" he answered. His voice was as large and sharp as a thunderstorm.

His voice scared the person on the other line. "Um... I'm sorry. Is this Tyreke Maxey?" he asked.

"Yes. This is him."

"Have I caught you at a bad time?" the person on the other line asked.

"No." Tyreke began to calm down as he sat back down in his seat. "May I ask whose calling?"

"This is Jerry Davis," he introduced, "president of the Florida Channel 23 News Station. I am here to talk about a temporary anchor position."

Before Tyreke married Eve, he interned at Channel 23 in Florida. Who knew that Mr. Davis remembered him. "Yes, I'm listening."

"Well, one of our anchors is on maternity leave," Mr. Davis concluded, "and we would like you to replace her for a few months. Are you interested?"

"Yes, sir! I am. *** I'll get back to you! *** Thank you." Tyreke hung up the phone. This was the opportunity he prayed for.

Tyreke boldly stood up out of his desk, and he walked up to Aaron's office door.

Knock! Knock! Knock!

Aaron opened the door with a disgusted look on his face. "What do you want, Mr. Maxey?"

"I would just like to inform you that I just got a call from Jerry Davis, president of Channel 23 in Florida." Tyreke smiled.

"I don't have time for your games, Maxey!" Aaron shouted with frustration. "Get to the point!"

"Mr. Davis called to inform me that they need a temporary replacement for an anchor whose on maternity leave. I just want to tell you that I'll be gone for the summer. I'll be back in the middle of August."

"No! You can't leave! I need you here for the summer," Aaron whined. "How can I leave for a summer vacation? I can't leave this place unsupervised."

"Get someone else that you don't care about to watch the place while you're gone. I'm going to Florida!"

"If you leave for the summer, you will not have a job when you return!" Aaron threatened. He thought he had Tyreke right where he wanted him.

But Tyreke just smiled. He felt as if a burden had been lifted off of him. Tyreke did not return a reply to Aaron's threat. Instead, he turned around and walked to his desk. He picked up his travel bag with his laptop, pens, and notebooks in it, and he walked over to Aaron and handed him his I.D. tag. "We shall meet again."

"If there's a God," Aaron replied with an evil stare, "we won't."

Tyreke walked over to the elevator and took a good look at the place one more time. He sighed. Memories. The good times he had with Francis and the other employees would always remain with him. The doors slid open. He walked in the elevator, and the elevator doors closed.

Chapter 35

Two weeks passed since Tyreke quit his job at *The Boss Chronicle*. During that time, Kayla graduated from high school with a 4.0 GPA. Little TJ also graduated--- from kindergarten. Tyreke moved his stuff out of his apartment and shipped it to Florida. Grace was promoted to the tenth grade; Skeeter was promoted to the twelfth grade. On a sadder note, Malik and Dee broke up. Teresa could not live with herself because she took her cousin's boyfriend and betrayed her trust. In result, she broke up with Silk.

Today was a sad day for the Maxey family. Rev. and Mrs. Maxey, Grace, Mary, Kayla, and Skeeter were standing in the living room waiting for Tyreke's departure. "It's not going to be the same without him," Mrs. Maxey said sobbing a motherly sob.

"He's only going to be gone for the summer," Rev. Maxey said trying to keep his own self from crying. During the worst moments in his life, he always held a positive composure.

"But what if he likes it there, and he moves to Florida for good?" Grace asked.

"Then, that's probably where God called him to be," Rev. Maxey replied.

Tyreke walked downstairs and stood beside his family. "Well," he said, "this is it."

Tears began to flood the room. "Let's have prayer before you leave," Rev. Maxey suggested.

"Wait!" While the family was grouping together, the newest member of the Maxwell household ran downstairs and joined the circle. "Tyreke, I know we don't really know each other, but I wish you the best of luck."

"Thank you," Tyreke smiled through the tears. "God bless you while you're here in America, buddy!"

The Maxwell family, including Ben Lorry, grouped tighter together and held hands. They bowed their heads, and Rev. Maxey whispered a short prayer for traveling grace for his son and thanked the Lord for blessing the family with Ben.

When Rev. Maxey finished, Tyreke slowly hugged his siblings, his mother, who was crying the loudest and the most, and his father. Then, the doorbell chimed.

"I'll get it," Grace volunteered. She broke up the clump and walked to the door. She opened it, and Eve, TJ, Tony, Tyrone, Faith, Malik, Cherie, and Kellie were standing at the door. "Come in!"

Tyreke's friends and TJ walked in, and Tyreke walked over to them. He looked at the face of his son. "I love you, Daddy!" TJ replied.

Tyreke could not help but cry as he embraced TJ. "I love

you, too, son. "Individually, Tyreke hugged Eve, Tony, Tyrone, Faith, Malik, Cherie, and Kellie. "I better go," he suggested. It was a good idea because if he did not go now, he would never leave. He looked back at his family and friends as they sobbed and waved goodbye. Tyreke uttered a soft goodbye and walked out the door closing the door behind him.

Chapter 36

A few hours later...

Tyreke pulled up in front of the centrally located townhouse. He opened the door of his BMW and looked up and down the large building. Tyreke sighed and walked up the stairs to his door.

He noticed the doormat on the ground and pulled it up to see that a bright, gold key was laying on the ground. He knelt down to pick it up and put the key in the hole. When the key unlocked the lock, he opened the door and walked in.

Darkness. Tyreke switched on the light switch. Bright lights were everywhere. What a massive place to live! He wondered how it would look with his furniture in it.

Then, he felt something vibrating his pant leg pocket. He pulled out his cellular phone and flipped it open. "Hello. *** Hi, Mommy! *** Yes, I got here safely. *** Everything's fine. *** No, my stuff isn't here yet. I'm going to pick it up after I leave the news station. *** I'll make sure I call you when I get home from work. *** Give everyone my love. *** Love you, too! *** Bye!" He hung up the phone.

Tyreke looked around his townhouse one more time. "I think I'm going to like this place." Tyreke smiled and opened the door. He walked out the door and headed to his first day of work at Channel 23.

About the Author

Karlton Tyrone Clay, at the time of this publication, is twenty-one years old and a junior at Georgia State University in Atlanta, GA. He is the son of Pastor Kenneth and Mrs. Sonya Clay and is the oldest of six children. Karlton had a normal childhood and a normal teenage life until he was diagnosed with leukemia at the age of 16 on March 18, 2002. In spite of his adversity, God healed him, and he was still able to graduate from his high school, John S. Davidson Fine Arts School, with a 90.0 GPA qualifying him to graduate with honors. Now that he is at Georgia State University, he is striving for excellence academically, spiritually, and socially.

Even though he is away at school, he is still very active at his home church, New Creation Christian Church, in Augusta, GA, where he is the director of mass communication and drama. He is also active in the college ministry of his watch care church, New Birth Missionary Baptist Church, where he is a member of the Outlet College Ministry and AXIS: the college worship team. He is also active at Georgia State University, where he is a member of the Alpha Lambda Delta Freshman Honor Society, the National Society for Collegiate Scholars, and a staff writer for the arts & entertainment newspaper *The Urbanite*. He is also the CEO and president of Victory Productions, which has produced several plays, short films, and currently producing the monthly internet drama *College Daze*. As he continues to grow and mature, he remembers to seek God for any decision that he makes to ensure that it is the right one.

www.ingramcontent.com/pod-product-compliance
Lightning Source LLC
Chambersburg PA
CBHW051835170626
46807CB00003B/1196